Raising Hope

Tina Toles

First Edition
Raising Hope
Copyright © 2014 Tina Toles

Editor:
Audrey Green, Founder/CEO
Chosen to Write Publishing LLC

Publisher:
Toles Publishing House
Cover designed by Doug Toles, Sr.
Library Of Congress Control Number
2012909216
Raising Hope: A Christian fiction novel
Written for Youth and Adults.

ISBN-13 978-0-9794387-8-3
ISBN-10 0-9794387-8-0

Printer:
Quinn's Printing Center
7900 Paragon Rd.
Dayton, Ohio 45459
Phone: 937-439-0991
Printed in the U.S.A.

Dedicated to the memory
of my Daughter
Lashawnda Reese
March 1971-February 1976

**Dedicated to the memory of the women
Who helped me to become
Who and what I am today!**

Loved and Sadly Missed!

*Mamie Wilson
1903-1997*

*Mary F. Smith
1926-1997*

*Elmina Smith
1928-1999*

*Irene M. Ford
1920-2004*

*Byrdie Toles-Williams
1923-2007*

Gone but not forgotten!

Dedicated to the memory of loved ones.
Gone but not forgotten!
We stand upon their shoulders.

Akida   Clay
Alice   Smith
Thomas   Smith
Mary   Smith
Robert   Smith
Ozell   Smith
Garfield   Smith
Elmina   Smith
Marvin   Smith
Coleman   Smith
Mary   Boykin
Percilla   Wyse
Katherine   Waters
Robert   Waters
Lashawnda   Reese
Jackie   Davis, Jr.
Terrance   Jenkins
Albert   Higgins
Dorothy   Higgins
Eric   Harrington
Harold   Harrington
Theodore   Anderson
Charles   Henderson, Sr.
Charles   Henderson, Jr.

A special thank you to my family and friends for their support and encouragement:

Tony Smith
Pam Smith
Gwen Sain
Shirley Boyd
Audrey Green
Eugenia Gumm
Brenda Davis
Carolyn Brown
Alisa Harrington
Robbie Harrington
Carmisha Cooper
Rita Payne & Family
James (Shirlean) McCombs
Jimmy (Donna) Payne
Larry (Sheila) Moore
Sherrie Fudge-Galloway
Jessica Muhammad
Carolyn (Don) Cook
Perry (Evelyn) Henderson
Mark (Pam) Davis
Tony (Helen) Booker
American Baptist Church
Lake View Terrace, CA

Sharon Nutt
Patricia Kirk
Yvonne Hall
Tonya Mathis
Terri Forest
Dawn Yantis
Carol Tolbert
Connie Melson
Katrina Paulding
Roberta Conner
Wilthea Mcguire

6

Special thanks to:

Kathy Jones
Daisy Torrence
Anna Mitchell
Trey (Nikki) Lee
Shirley Wilkerson
Andre (Sherri) Ballard
Vicky Waters & Family
Christina (Darren) Mabrey
Lanisa Jenkins & Family
Pat Coleman, Godmother
Eddie (Notoshia) Howard
Sharon (Everett) Plummer
Ernestine Beasley & Family
Vincent (Sheila) Harrington
Gary (Sheila) Harris & Family
Eric, Lisa, Patrick Harrington
Stanley & Dwight Smith
Shiloh Baptist Church Family
Corinthian Baptist Church Family
Barnell (Willa) Hampton, Godparents
Arthur & Charlotte, Raymond Mcguire
Lynette Soil, Kitty Scoggins & Lawana Cooper
Janiece, Jennifer & Jonathan Jenkins, Jacques Davis

Special thanks to Members of the Dayton Christian Writers' Guild Inc.

Sharon Smith
Patrica Woods
Justine Nettleton
Eugenia Gumm
Audrey Green
Christina Mabrey
Judith Dammons
Melissa Richardson

This book is dedicated to my children, grandchildren, great-grandchildren and my godchildren. I want you to know how proud I am of all of you and I love you.

Children
Doug Toles Jr.
Sidney Smith
Tia (Justen) Seay
Mia Toles-Pickard
Dwayne (Charm) Toles
Stanley (Tashia) Reese

God children
Maria Clark
Bryan   George
Serina   Grove
Christina Tellis-Mabrey
Aniya & Aleah Lee
Amanda Macintosh

Grandchildren
Jay Storm
Devanni Toles
Deacon Seay
Paris Pickard
Mackenzie Reese
Raymond Jordon
Taneishia Hunter
Jordan Valentine
Cameron Lucas-Toles
Mickeyen Fitzpatrick
Carmen (Roosevelt) Dixon
Deduria (Kenyuan) Cornelious

Great-Grandchildren
Arick White
Jaidyn Storm
Darren Morrow Jr.
Danielle, DaLeon Cotton
Kayla, Dariyuan Kayceon Cornelious

To My Wife, Tina Toles

In the beginning of our relationship many people had negative things to say. However, I didn't hear their words, because, I believed then and now that a person should have an opportunity to prove themselves. I also believed that love can change a person and I loved you the first time I kissed your lips. Therefore, I listened to my heart and fell deeply in love with you. I let God lead and guide me and I'm so happy that I did, because they were wrong.

When we met, you were indeed a diamond in the rough and, you have become an one-caret diamond, that I am honored to call my wife. You are beautiful inside and out. I have watched you mature and become a woman of God. You have made my life heaven here on earth. I thank God for placing you in my life. You are an exceptional wife, mother, grandmother and educator. You are a virtuous woman of God and, we are blessed to have you in our lives.

You have taught me the true meaning of unconditional love and for that I thank you. Having you in my life has made me feel like the luckiest man in the world. I look forward to loving you until death do us part. I pray God blesses us with many, many more years of love and happiness.

Congratulations on your new novel, I have enjoyed reading your novels. I am so proud of you. Keep on allowing God to use you and God will bless you abundantly.

Your Husband,
Doug Toles

Personal Reflections

This story of friends and family reminds me there are always challenges in every family at any given point of time. Through thick and thin, for better for worse, we triumph by believing that God never gives us more than we can handle. That it is not our place to worry. It is our place to believe in the power of God and His will upon men.

Dawn Yantis, Secretary
Northmont High School

Personal Reflections

The story of Destiny and Hope continues. We see Hope as a teenager and the problems she and her family encounter at that critical stage of her life. In this sequel Tina Toles exhibits her continuing story telling expertise. She does not disappoint us as the story of the family unfolds. You will be pulled in and held to the very end. It is a pleasure to see Tina Toles continue to develop as a novelist.

Sharon Nutt,
Simply Reading Book Club

Personal Reflections

Congratulations Tina, you have taken the challenge to become a storyteller in your work. You have crafted this novel and created characters who endure life's struggles to survive and exist with a lot of prayers and hope. This book weaves dreams of social uplifting, courage, communication, family members and love ones.

Tina Toles has grown from writing poetry to a very compelling novel. She has woven a fast pace read confronting most of the issues and concerns we face in everyday life. Each character highlights an area of importance such as; pain, illness, sorrow, suicide, death, Cancer, bullying, strokes, loneliness and empowerment.

Although this is a fiction novel, current up-to-date data and statistic empower the subject at hand such as; (43% kid's say they have been bullied verbally online, 80% of today's children use cell phones and 85% of teens today believe cyber bullying is a serious problem). This novel also explains in detail what causes Post-Traumatic Stress Disorder (PTSD) in our war veterans.

I would say this novel is "Effective and Incredibly Practical". It meets people at all different places and it makes them think. Tina keep reaching for the STARS!

Dr. Connie Melson, Retired Librarian
Dayton Metro Library
Madden Hills Branch

Personal Reflections

A timely series of episodes for such a time as this in today's society. Individual,individuals are in the need of hope and love, which may include disappointments, as well as, corrections to bring about making clear decisions for a bright future.

Hope experiences had lead her to gain more strength, and knowledge furthermore, wisdom which shines in her heart. Alongside, she learns how to rely on God each and everyday.

Tina, has a keen ear to hear from God in which He has placed in her heart to write and reach individual,individuals who are in need of answers and deliverance.

Thank you, Tina Toles for obeying God to write for His Glory, to inspire individual,individuals lives. May God continue to enrich you more in Him.

Dr. Eugenia Gumm, Vice-President
Dayton Christian Writers' Guild Inc.

Personal Reflections

Tina Toles is earning a reputation as a masterful storyteller with a fresh lyrical and reverent voice. Once again, she has proven not only can she compose poetry but, she can pen a compelling novel.

"Raising Hope" is a story that celebrates the power of faith and it chronicles the struggles of a troubled teenager who endures tragedy and pain. Through the character Hope Chandler-Washington, Tina Toles inspires us to fight our way through life struggles and never give up.

Every Christian, parent and child should read this fictional narrative. Whatever you do, don't loan this book out, because you'll never get it back.

Rev. Dr. P. E. Henderson, Jr., Pastor
Corinthian Baptist Church

Dayton Christian Writers' Guild Inc.

The Dayton Christian Writers' Guild Inc., was organized in September 1993 under the leadership of Mrs. Tina Toles. The Writers' Guild is a 501-3(C) organization. Our goal is to minister through our writing. Our objective is to write for God's glory. Our mission is to educate, teach, and train others who have a desire to use their God-given ability to write for God's Glory. The Writers' Guild is a support group for Christians who feel God has given them a special gift or talent to write for His Glory. We are a fellowship and information group for novice and professional writers. We invite both novice and experienced writers to become active members. We also invite those with a desire to write, but who have not yet accomplished their mission to join us. We want to support Christians who feel called by God to develop their talents and to share their knowledge with others. We are individual, individuals who want to grow spiritually, to provide inspiration, and to give God the glory. We inspire to become better stewards of God's gift. We meet at Corinthian Baptist Church, 700 S. James McGee Blvd., 2:00 p.m., the second Saturday of every month. Please come join us and bring a friend!

Tina Toles, Founder/President
Dayton Christian Writers' Guild Inc.

Reflections From The Author

Raising Hope is a christian fiction novel. This situation seems ever so real, at times I had to remind myself it was a work of fiction given by God. He placed it in my spirit to share with those who believe and love Him. The characters took a life of their own. Fiction does in many ways mimic life. Many christians believe that because they have given their lives to Christ nothing negative or evil will happen to them and that is just not true. Many times, as christians, our faith is put to a test. During our trials and tribulations, it is then that we find out if our faith in God is shallow or if our faith in God is deep and can withstand any test that is thrown at us. He is always near to comfort us and lead us through our toughest situation.

In God's Word, we are told the "Faith of a tiny mustard seed we can move mountains." Because of Gwen's faith in God, Hope learns that she can in fact, be successful by having faith in God for herself. We as christians, can learn a valuable lesson through watching Hope's life unravel. When things look their worse, God steps in to show Hope favor. Hope also learns a lesson that we should all learn, family is not about blood rather it's about who's willing to hold your hand when you need it the most. Family are the ones willing to love you unconditionally. Family and friends are a blessing from God.

To God Be The Glory!

Prologue

Hope is an angry teenager who is mad at the world because she feels life isn't fair. She is angry with God because her life has been so hard. She has to deal with the death of a loved one, at a time in her life when she should be happy and excited about her future, which only fuels her anger and hatred of society.

She doesn't like her stepfather just because he's in law enforcement. She feels her mother is being controlled by her stepfather. The only good thing about her life is her little brother Daniel, Jr., whom she adores.

Hope grows up on this journey and learns to have faith in God and faith in herself. She also learns that the word "family" doesn't just apply to blood relatives.

She learns that there are still good people in our society, and they will help you in your hour of need, asking for nothing in return.

Contents

Dedication   3
In Memory   4
In Memory Of Family   5
Special Thanks   6
Dayton Christian Writers' Members   8
Dedication To Family   9
A Letter From My Husband   10
Dawn Yantis   11
Sharon Nutt   12
Connie Lucas-Melson   13
Eugenia Gumm   14
P. E Henderson Jr.   15
Dayton Christian Writers' History   16
Reflections From The Author   17
Prologue   18
Chapter   1   Hope's High School Troubles   21
Chapter   2   Gwen's Health Scare   26
Chapter   3   Daniel, Sr., A Brush With Death   34
Chapter   4   Suspect Captured   42
Chapter   5   Hope's Graduation   49
Chapter   6   Hope's Pain and Despair   58
Chapter   7   Daniel, Jr's Troubles   66
Chapter   8   Daniel, Jr., Faces His Bully   74
Chapter   9   Sweet Revenge   80
Chapter   10   A Visit To The White House   90
Chapter   11   Daniel Jr. Returns To School   96
Chapter   12   School Board Found Guilty   101
Chapter   13   Destiny Has Breast Cancer   108
Chapter   14   Terry, Sr., Has A Family Crisis   114
Chapter   15   Flight To Atlanta   121
Chapter   16   Marion's Health Declines   127

Contents

Chapter   17   Terry, Sr. Faces A Dilemma   133
Chapter   18   A New Birth   140
Chapter   19   Terry, Sr., Finds Peace   147
Chapter   20   Terry, Sr., and Gwen Find Love   154
Books published by Toles Publishing House   160
Books by the Author   161
Books by Dayton Christian Writers' Guild   162

Chapter One
Hope's High School Troubles

One

Hope Chandler-Washington is my given name. I am sixteen years old. Sixteen is a magical number or so I've been told. It should be one of the happiest years of my life. However, it's not. In fact, I am so unhappy I wonder if there is a God? I wonder why doesn't He let me die? My mother, Destiny and my stepfather, Daniel try so hard to make me happy, but with no success. My whole world is dark and gloomy because of one person, Tyrone. He's sixteen and attends school with me, Paul L Dunbar High School. Tyrone is shorter than me, but I don't care. He's about 5'7 and he weighs about two-hundred pounds. He has a body that looks like he could win first place in a body building competition. All that doesn't matter because I love him. My whole world is falling apart because I thought that he loved me and he doesn't, he lied. It's homecoming week at the high school.

Tyrone was to be my date. I am so excited about going to the homecoming dance with Tyrone. He brought me flowers and seemed to be excited about going to the dance However, it was really just a cruel joke! I bought this beautiful red dress, with matching red shoes that had four inch heels. My mother bought me the jewelry to match. I looked beautiful if I must say so. I am 5'10 with a shape like an hour glass. I have flowing black hair down my back. The boy's at school would whistle when they saw me walking down the hallway. But, I have eyes only for Tyrone, he holds the key to my heart.

It's Saturday, the night I have dreamt about for months. I'm dressed and sitting at the front door waiting for Tyrone. The dance is to start at seven this evening. It's four, five and then six o'clock and still no, Tyrone. I sit by the window looking out patiently for hours and still no, Tyrone. I keep saying to myself, "he's just running late." I even tell my mother "he's just running late, he'll be here. But no, that isn't the case. When I finally realize he isn't coming I cry as if the world is coming to an end and for me it is. My mother tries to comfort me, but she can't. All I can think about is Tyrone. He doesn't love me and I just want to die. He is my whole reason for living. My world revolves around Tyrone and nothing else matters. Day after day I sit by the phone waiting for Tyrone to call. I'm sure there's a good reason for his not showing up to take me to the dance. For days I wouldn't eat or sleep. I wouldn't leave my room. My stepfather, kept saying,

"You're to young to feel this way about a boy, this is silly. You need to move on with your life. It only made me mad to hear him say those words. I thought "Why doesn't he just shut up, get out and just leave me alone." Mother and my stepfather are having problems because they can't agree on how to deal with my crisis. My stepfather wants to send me to a school for troubled youth. I think he just wants to get rid of me. I'm just a thorn in his side. My mother thinks if we pray and seek spiritual help things will improve. That's the answer to all her problems. That's a mother's job to have faith in God and her family.

Seeing Tyrone everyday only makes me feel worse. He didn't even apologize or make up an excuse for not showing up. Everytime I see him I want to cut him. Anger kepts building up day after day, I just can't seem to control myself. So I decide to act on my feelings. I pulled from my pocket a rat tail comb and when I saw him a little voice in my head said, "stab him" he deserves to bleed a little. So I did just that. When I stabbed him and his blood started flowing he looked so shocked. Then, he had the nerve to look up at me and asked me why I stabbed him. Which only made me want to stab him again. The school nurse was called and she responded quickly. She was able to stop the bleeding since the cut wasn't very deep. Tyrone was taken to the hospital and he was discharged after an hour. I was suspened from school. But I didn't care I hated school. I had to go to court and the judge ordered us into family counseling. Stabbing Tyrone only made me feel worse. I'm on an emotional roller coaster ride that's on a collision course. I can't shake those deep dark feelings, so I cut my wrist. My mother found me bleeding on the bathroom floor. I was rushed to the hospital. I awoke the next day to find myself in the hospital strapped to a gurney. With my mother, stepfather, grandmother and my brother standing at the foot of my bed. I burst into tears realizing all the pain I have caused them.

I was released after three days into the custody of my parents. Family counseling was again ordered. I didn't go to jail because Tyrone didn't press charges. I was placed on probation for a year with mandatory counseling. The judge placed a restraining order on me, which stated I was to stay 100 feet away from Tyrone. I didn't care because I never wanted to see Tyrone ever again.

With anger management counseling and the support from my family in the days and weeks ahead I began to feel better. I still had a long road ahead of me to a full and complete recovery. But, I was back on the road to living a normal life. I have learned a valuable lesson "That nothing is worth taking your own life." If you seek professional help and take things one day at a time things will get better.

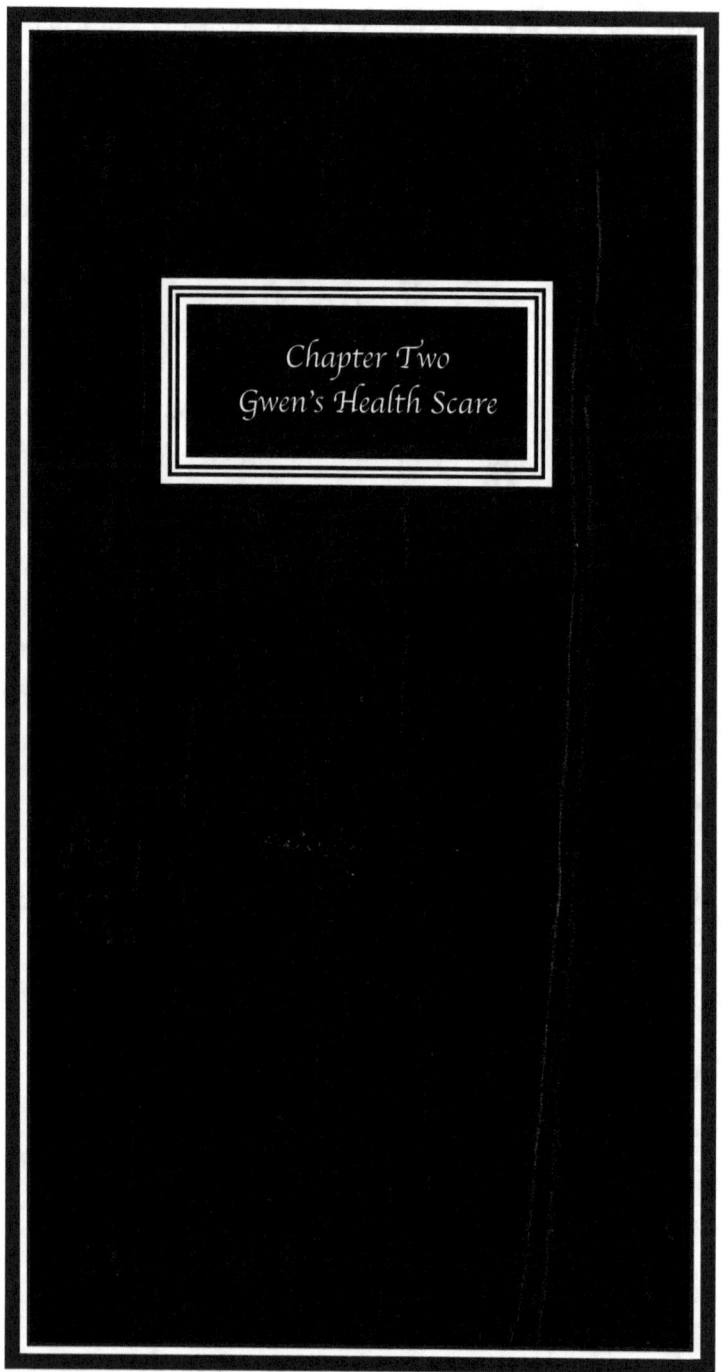

Chapter Two
Gwen's Health Scare

Two

Unable to accept her husband's death my grandmother had a mental break down. Thus, the shelter that she owned had to be closed. My grandmother had a full recovery however, she decided to retire. Her job now is to be a grandmother and caregiver for me and my little brother. She takes us to school and picks us up. She attends our school activities and Parent Teacher Association, (P. T. A.) meetings. If we are sick and can't go to school we stay with my grandmother while mom and my stepfather worked. Mom works as a dispatcher at the patrol station. My stepfather has been promoted to captain at the highway patrol station. He has worked for the highway patrol for over twenty years.

Being with my grandmother is the only time I can remember being happy and feeling good. My grandmother was the one person that I could talk to, she understands me. My grandmother's life revolves around me and her church.

She never dated or showed interest in anyone after her husband, David passed. When asked, she would reply "my heart died when David's heart stopped beating". He was her first and only love and she was okay with that. The only love that she needed she receives from me and my brother Daniel, Jr., Those words always put a smile on my face. My grandmother was now sixty years old. She could pass for thirty. She exercised and walks daily until now. She had not had any health issues. So the call from the neighbor that said, 'my grandmother had been rushed to the hospital', caught us all by surprise. We just couldn't imagine what could be wrong. Mom was screaming at the top of her lungs, "Let's go." We need to get to the hospital. My stepfather, drove recklessly to get there. The car was silent except for the squealing of tires. My heart was racing from fear and my stepfather's driving. Even though my stepfather was driving over the speed limit, it seemed to take forever to get there. Upon arrival my stepfather flashed his badge so he would be taken to my grandmother's room. My stepfather told us to take a seat in the waiting room and that he would return when he got more information.

My mother wasn't happy with that and neither was I but, we did as instructed. Mom sat down and started to pray. Feeling restless and worried we were unable to sit down, so my brother, and I walked the floor until our feet hurt. I couldn't help but think about all the cookies she had baked and all the hugs and kisses she had given me when I was sick. The many meals she had cooked and the many hours we spent playing games. My grandmother just couldn't be sick and dying because, I hadn't told her how much she meant to me or how much I loved her. I didn't know much about God or praying but, I thought this might be a good time to try. "God if You're listening, I'm not sure why You would be because, I'm a sinner, but if You're listening I need to asked You a favor. Please spare my grandmother's life, heal her body. If You do I'll go to Church. I'll even be a better person. I'll even be nicer to my little brother. Please God make her whole again."

My stepfather returned to the surgery waiting room to share grandmother's condition. Upon seeing her husband's face, mom fell into his arms sobb. My stepfather, gently guided mom to a seat. Then he informed us that the doctor was still running tests and the final results were not available. He didn't want to give us false hope and he didn't want us to get needlessly upset. However, the doctor believed my grandmother had suffered a stroke on her left side due to a blood clot. The doctor believed she was going to be okay but, it would take some time. She would need months of therapy. The stroke affected her left side. My grandmother couldn't move her left arm or speak. She had been taken into surgery to repair the damage. The doctor informed us she could have visitors once she was out of recovery. All we could do now is pray. Mom burst into tears and so did I. These were tears of relief that God had spared my grandmother's life. We stood in the waiting room hugging, crying and kissing each other. Mom stopped crying and asked that we all join hands to give thanks to God for the miracle that had just taken place and for the complete healing of grandmother's body. When she finished I started praying. This shocked everyone but, it was the first of many prayers I would offer to God.

My grandmother was in recovery and things had calmed down. Mom called Terry, Sr., David's brother and shared with him the tragic news. He was on the next flight to Dayton. Terry, Sr., arrived within a couple of hours. We met him at the airport. Terry, Sr., lives in Atlanta, Georgia with his family. We had not seen Terry, Sr., in several years. We had communicated through cards, e-mail and phone calls. However, Terry, Sr., had not changed. He was still handsome and tall with pearly white teeth. He had a beautiful bronze complexion. His skin was so tanned he looked like he had been on vacation in Jamaica. He had aged gracefully. Every hair on his head was now gray. He had a few extra pounds around his mid-section. However, he was still a pleasant vision to lay eyes upon. Terry, Sr., greeted us with hugs, kisses and a big smile. But it was obvious he was worried about something his eyes looked sad. I wondered if his sadness was about my grandmother or if something else was troubling him. I hoped I would know the answer before he left. We took Terry, Sr., directly to the hospital. my stepfather explained my grandmother condition as he drove. We arrived at the hospital after visiting hours. However, the hospital staff allowed us to have a brief visit because Terry, Sr., lived out of state. Mom went in first to inform my grandmother that she had an unexpected visitor. She was careful not to call Terry's name. Mom wanted to see if my grandmother would recognize her visitor at first sight and would be able to recall his name. Mom kissed my grandmother on the forehead and left to allow Terry, Sr., to visit. He stood in the doorway not sure of what his eyes would behold. He smiled, and slowly went to be by her bedside. Terry, Sr., was nervous and worried about the damage the stroke had done. Looking into her eyes brought back pleasant memories. My grandmother's face lit up, when Terry, Sr., entered. She did remember him and wondered what he had been doing since the last time she had seen him. Unable to speak the answers to those questions would have to wait.

My grandmother was still a beautiful woman. She was small in stature only 5'2', and that was with high heels on. She weighed 100 pounds soaking wet. With jet black hair that now has turned completely gray. She has eyes that could melt your heart. He remembered her as a strong willed, explosive, opinionated beautiful woman. My grandmother was as beautiful as he had remembered. She extended her right hand and tried to call out his name. But the stroke had temporarily limited her speech and movement on the left side. My grandmother smiled as tears ran down the side of her face.

Terry, Sr., took her hand and kissed her forehead trying to comfort her and assure her everything was going to be alright. He spoke softly trying to reassure her that he wouldn't leave her bedside until her health returned. Terry, Sr., kept his word he remained by my grandmother's bedside 24/7 for three months. I believe my grandmother's recovery was due to Terry's love and support. The doctor's were amazed at her recovery. Within the first month my grandmother was able to feed herself. During the second month she was talking and making jokes. By the end of the third month my grandmother was up and walking around the hospital without any assistance. My grandmother returned home after three months of therapy looking as if nothing had happened. My grandmother and Terry, Sr., were close before the stroke but, now they were even closer. My grandmother had recovered and Terry's job was finished, now it was time for him to return home to see about his family. My grandmother felt sad that he was leaving, however, she knew their time together had to come to an end. My grandmother took him to the airport. There they said their good byes.

Our lives returned to normal however, there were a few important changes in my life. I made a promise to God and I intended to keep my word. I worked hard at school and I was on the honor roll. My home life was great. I joined my grandmother's church and I'm on the usher board. This made my parents and my grandmother extremely happy. I am attending bible study on Wednesday nights. Even singing in the choir for women's day and special occasions. My brother made fun of me. Telling everyone that I couldn't sing, that I was just lip syncing. That was until the church choir had a concert and I had to lead a song, written by Kirk Franklin, titled, "Smile". If I must say so, I sang that song like a professional. I went straight to my brother and looked him in his eyes and said, "Now who did you say couldn't sing?" He had to give me a little respect after that performance. I told everyone I was going to try out for "American

Idol" next season. Of course, I wasn't telling the truth. I just wanted to see the look on my little brother's face. I laughed until I cried. It was priceless. I wish I had a camera to capture the moment. However, I'll never forget the day I broke his face. It felt so good.

Mom and my stepfather are wondering what or who has taken over my body. Because I'm smiling and happy. No more voices or dark thoughts, and my attitude about life and God has changed.

I have new friends and a social life. I met a young man at church and he likes me. We're taking things slow. We have our first date on Saturday. It's the first prom I've attended and probably my last since I'm a senior this year. My brother is now in high school and he's having the time of his life. I'm so proud of him.

Chapter Thre
Daniel, Sr., A Brush With Death

Three

Mom and stepfather are celebrating their twentieth anniversary next month. They are planning a big celebration and a return trip to Jamaica, this time without any children. Mom was so happy and excited about their anniversary and their trip. Their plans were almost finalized when mom's dreams were crushed. There was a knock at the front door. Mom opened it to find two of my stepfather's fellow officer's standing at the door. Mom smiled and greeted them with a big hug. They returned her hug but, they were not smiling. Mom took a step back realizing this was not a social call. Fear gripped her heart and her heart started racing. She grabbed at her chest because, she couldn't catch her breath. One of the officers took her by the hand and lead her to a seat in the living room.

Finally, mom said, "Where is my husband? What has happened?" The officer stated, "There's been an accident, and we have come to escort the family to the hospital."Mom, started sobbing. Between tears she asked, "Is he alright? She demanded they tell her right now? Is he alright?" The officer lowered his head and said, "We don't know how bad it is. We were just told to pick up his family and get them to the hospital. You need to talk with the doctors at the hospital they can explain his condition." Mom quickly gathered her things and headed to the cruiser that was waiting. She asked if they could make a stop at the High School to pick up me and my brother. We were paged to the Principal's office and mom was waiting out in the hallway. Upon seeing mom's face, we knew something was wrong but, we thought it was my grandmother in crisis. Much to our surprise, it was my stepfather.

My stepfather went to work as usual however, this was not a routine or typical day. He was patrolling on I-75 and stopped a car for speeding. The driver seemed annoyed and stressed out at being stopped. The driver was a typical white male with blue eyes and blonde hair. He looked to be about nineteen. Fresh out of high school or maybe his first year of college. He didn't look to be a threat, so thought my stepfather. However, he was wrong. My stepfather asked to see the youngman's identification and proof of insurance. The youngman said, "Yes, sir officer" and he reached into his glove compartment with a smile on his face. He pulled out a .38 revolver and shot my stepfather one time and drove off. My stepfather was able to call for backup before

36

he passed out. When backup arrived, they found my stepfather on the ground with a bullet in his left shoulder. He was bleeding profusely from his shoulder wound. He passed out due to his blood loss. When an officer is in trouble, a signal 99 goes out over the patrol officer's radio. An "All Points bulletin" was put out for the young man and the make and model of his car. The A.P.B. stated the young man was armed and dangerous, approach with caution. The EMT's arrived quickly knowing a fellow officer was down. My stepfather was rushed to Grandview Hospital. He regained consciousness briefly in route to the hospital. He asked the EMT's if his wife and family had been called and then he loss consciousness before the reply was given.

Mom, my grandmother, my brother and I reached the hospital just in time to see my stepfather being taken into the hospital entrance. Mom shouted,"Stop that's my husband". The attendant slowed down for a brief moment. Just long enough for us to see his face and for mom to plant a kiss on his lips. Then she whispered, "I love you" before she broke down into tears. A state trooper wrapped his arms around mom and guided her to the hospital waiting room, we followed close behind them. He instructed us to wait here and he would check on the captian for us. Mom sat starring into space and rocking back and forth. I wanted to comfort her, but I didn't know what to do or say, so I prayed. My stepfather had been rushed into surgery. He had loss a lot of blood before the EMT's arrived. No one had spoken to us regarding the severity of his condition. Mom and my grandmother were growing impatient and worried. They were also concerned because they thought he might lose his arm, be paralyzed or even die due to his injuries. Seven hours and still no news on my stepfather'scondition. Mom, prayed and cried, prayed and cried some more. Finally, a doctor appeared in the waiting room and asked for the family of Daniel Washington. Everyone in the waiting room stood up. News had spread fast of the shooting and the entire community had come out for support. Plus, his buddies from the patrol station and state trooper from all over the state had come to pray and to offer their support. I had to wonder who was watching and protecting the community? Because it looked like every trooper from miles around was sitting or standing in the hospital waiting room. The doctor looked around at all the worried faces. Finally, he said, "I need to talk with Washington's immediate family, wife, mother or children." Mom stood to her feet and greeted the doctor. I am Mrs. Washington, and whatever you need to say to me can be said to everyone in this room. Because they are family and they love my husband as much as I do. With that being said, the doctor informed us Captain Washington is in recovery. The room erupted into cheers and high-fives. The doctor waited for things to settle down, then he continued. Captain Washington survived the surgery and that's good. However, he's not out of danger. He survived because he was in such good physical shape. His weight lifting and gym activities may have saved his life. He's still unconscious and we won't know the full extent of the damage until he's awake.

The good news is that we were able to save his arm. We were concerned that he may have suffered some nerve damage due to where the bullet struck him. This will be revealed in his therapy session. The room erupted again. This time a nurse entered the room. The look on her face told us she wasn't happy about the noise we were making. She put her hands on her hips and in a very stern voice she reminded us that this was a hospital with sick people. We needed to quiet down or she would have security remove everyone except the wife. The cheering stopped and the doctor continued. Captain Washington will be in the hospital for several months and he may need additional surgeries and extensive therapy. Mom took a seat feeling a bit overwhelmed with the information the doctor had shared. After she gathered her thoughts she instructed us to form a circle and we began to pray thanking God for sparing his life. No matter how long it took she would be by his side.

As it grew late into the night friends and family started leaving. That's when mom realized she had not contacted her husbands family. Which included Denzel Washington, Daniel's first cousin. Mom started the tedious task of contacting her husbands family. Those she couldn't reach she left messages for them to contact her.

Mom also called her brother-in-law, Terry to share the tragic news with him and his family. Mom refused to leave her husbands hospital room. She wouldn't eat or drink anything. My grandmother was worried about both of them, but there was nothing she could do for either of them. My grandmother said a prayer, then took me and my brother to her house so we could get a bit to eat and some sleep. We left mom sitting beside his bed, watching him as he slept. Mom was worried because he had not regained consciousness. Mom just wanted to see him open his big beautiful brown eyes and she would know he was really okay. But, he continued to sleep through the night. Bright and early the next morning his eyes opened to see his wife sleeping in a chair next to his bed. He watched as she slept. She looked tired and uncomfortable in the chair she was sleeping in but he let her sleep. My stepfather lay in bed rethinking the events that put him in this hospital bed. He couldn't believe that after serving over twenty years on the force, he had been shot by some spoiled little white kid. He questioned his actions and wondered if he had done something wrong. But, before he could figure it out he heard his wife's voice. She saw that he was awake and she started hugging and kissing him. She said a silent prayer thanking God for sparing her husband's life. He was trying in vain to convince his wife it was just a simple flesh wound and he was okay. Mom just wasn't buying it. The doctor's words were still ringing in her ears. She knew they still had a rough road ahead. My stepfather wasn't a young man anymore and his body would take longer to heal. Trying to get my stepfather to accept that fact was an impossible task. Mom knew keeping her husband still was going to take a miracle. He hated resting or relaxing. My stepfather always said, "He would have plenty of time to relax when he was six feet under. As long as his body was able, he intended to work and work hard, he did".

Mom was worried that her husband, my stepfather would work himself to death and drop dead of a heart attack on the job. Since he didn't know the words relax or vacation. Mom refused to accept his attitude, about working till you die. She continued to try to convince him that everyone needs to rest and take some vacation time. Her words fell on death ears.

Chapter Four
Suspect Captured

FOUR

My stepfather was released from the hospital thirty days later. He was told to report to outpatient therapy for four weeks. Then, he could return to work if cleared by the staff psychologist. My stepfather got excited when he heard the words "return to work". Mom had to remind him that he couldn't return to work until his therapy was complete. My stepfather was discharged and mom drove him home. When they arrived at the house there was a banner in the front yard which read "Welcome Home Captain Washington." When the door to the house opened, the living room was full to capacity with family and friends all happy to see him home. His arm was in a sling and he had limited mobility but yet, he wasn't in any pain.

Mom took care of my stepfather's every need. She drove him back and forth to therapy everyday and truly enjoyed being in charge. She hated to think about him returning to work. However, she knew that day was fast approaching. My stepfather was not only improving, he was lifting weights and jogging a few miles each day. Today was his last day in therapy. He had a doctor's appointment and he expected the doctor to release him to return to duty. Mom was nervous about him returning because the fool that shot him had not been captured. But it didn't seem to bother him in the least. He loved his job and was excited about returning to work. The day before he was to return to work he was sitting in the kitchen listening to the police scanner when he heard, "All units we have spotted a vehicle and suspect who is speeding and believed to have assaulted a fellow officer. All available units please assist in the suspect pursuit and capture". My stepfather started pacing the floor. He was ready to join in on the chase. Mom had to take the car keys from his hand and remind him that he had not been released for duty yet. He argued that he felt fine and that the doctor's would release him tomorrow. Mom shook her head no and that was final. Your buddies will catch him. My stepfather sat back down with a frown on his face because he knew mom was right. He returned to listening to the police scanner. The suspect had been cornered, but he wasn't giving up easily. My stepfather was yelling at the police scanner and hitting the counter at the same time. He yelled, "Pull out the tear gas and gas his butt". He was yelling as if they heard him. When mom saw the expression on his face she had to laugh however, my stepfather didn't find any humor in the situation. He thought they were making all kinds of errors. The troopers did eventually throw tear gas at the suspect. When all attempts failed to get him to surrender peacefully. The suspect screamed and hollered like a little girl when he came in contact with the tear gas. Once he was taken into custody and placed in the cruiser his car was searched. They found drugs and a weapons. That's why he hadn't wanted to stop when the troopers turned their lights on. When the suspect was processed and booked he was placed in a line-up. My stepfather was asked to identify his attacker. He was happy to assist in identifying the perpetrator. This was indeed the young man who had tried to take his life. When asked why he shot Officer Washington he replied, "I already have two strikes against me for selling drugs, and if I get busted again this would be my third strike. According to California law he would be sent to prison for life. California is where he lived and grew up. He was in Ohio visiting family members. He was willing to kill rather than be sent to jail again. He pleaded not guilty. His trial was set for next year. My stepfather was not happy about the trial being held next year. He wanted his perpetrator sitting in jail for life now. We would have to wait to see if he get justice.

My stepfather returned to work and so did mom. However, things have not returned to normal. My stepfather was having nightmares about the shooting, so he doesn't want to sleep. Mom is afraid because my stepfather becomes very violent and forceful in his sleep. He seems to be mad at the world. Mom and my stepfather are fighting all the time. Mom has asked, my stepfather to get counseling, but he refuses. My stepfather seems to think there's nothing wrong with him. He thinks he's just having trouble sleeping and that he can handle this on his own. My stepfather says, "Seeing a head doctor is a waste of time and money." They just take your money and waste your time. He has better things to do with his time and his money.

It breaks my heart to see mom so frustrated and unhappy. She is again doing the only thing she knows to do and that's pray and cry, and then pray and cry some more. Mom's at the end of her rope so she turns to her Pastor for help and counseling. My stepfather is not happy about that either. "This is family business and what happens in this house stays within these four walls." However, mom feels as if she doesn't talk to someone she is going to lose her mind. She tries to get my stepfather to come to the counseling sessions with her but again, it only makes my stepfather furious, so mom goes alone. My mother's pastor listened as she poured out her heart. Describing her husbands behavior, sobbing and crying throughout her session. Once she finished Pastor Davis started praying. He prayed for twenty minutes, "I believe your husband is experiencing what is commonly known as post traumatic stress disorder, or PTSD." He has experienced a severe trauma and life-threatening event. Some of the signs of PTSD are you feel on edge. Nightmares keep coming back. Sudden noises make you jump. Other symptoms of PTSD include sleeplessness, loss of interest, or feeling numb, anger and irritability. But there are many ways PTSD can impact your everyday life. Sometimes these symptoms don't surface for months or years after the event. The symptoms vary and may also come and go. Her pastor also stated that my stepfather feels like our lives and the lives of your children are in danger. He has no control over what is happening. Which can only compound his stress level. Some other signs of PTSD are that he may start drinking or using drugs to numb his feelings. He says, my stepfather may also consider harming himself or others. He may start working all the time to occupy his mind. He may also pull away from other people and become isolated. The first step in healing is to realize there is a problem. The second step is wanting to be whole again. Your husband, Captain Washington, is in trouble and needs counseling and medication. Because he has PTSD, doesn't mean he just has to live with it. In recent years, research from around the world has dramatically increased our understanding of what causes PTSD and how to treat it. Hundreds of thousands of veterans have gotten treatment for PTSD— and the treatment works. There are two types of treatment that have been shown to be effective for treating PTSD: counseling and medication. Professional counseling can help him understand his thoughts and discover ways to cope with his feelings. Medications, called selective serotonin re-uptake inhibitors, are used to help him feel less worried or sad. In just a few months, these treatments can produce positive and meaningful changes in symptoms and his quality of life. They can help your husband understand his PTSD and change how he thinks about his trauma—and change how he reacts to stressful memories. But, again I repeat, he must want to change his life. It is my prayer that he will find healing and perfect peace. Mom thanked her pastor and left feeling optimistic about their future.

Chapter Five
Hope's Graduation

FIVE

My senior year was coming to an end fast. Time had moved so swiftly. However, I'm ready to move on with my life. Which means leaving the comforts of my parents home and going to college. During the last nine months I have matured quickly, because of the various challenges I've had to endure, but I'm not complaining. I've learned to believe in myself and in God. I've learned love begins within. To receive love you must be willing to give love in return. Which also means you must be willing to take a chance that you heart may be broken.

I am making preparations to graduate from high school. So many things need to be done. I have been asked to be valedictorianformyclass.MyG.P.A.isratedwithinthetopten percentofmyclass. I neverthoughtthiswould happen to me. I didn't think my life could or would change so drastically.

Things have started falling into place. I am attending my senior prom with one of the young men from my church. Bruce and I were voted king and queen of the homecoming Court. We both received a thousand-dollar scholarship package to a college of our choice, because we both have 4.0 GPA's. A big banquet and parade was held in our honor. Bruce picked me up in a black limo. He presented me with a dozen roses. Then, he blew me away when he asked if we could continue to date as boyfriend and girlfriend. Bruce also stated he had deep feelings for me and he hoped I felt the same way. I was just so shocked and speechless. I couldn't find the words to express how happy I was. Leaving high school will be bitter sweet.

Graduation day is here. I've picked up my cap and gown. The graduation ceremony is tonight. I have butterflies in my stomach. I've written a farewell speech and I have read it over and over again. I'm so afraid I'll pass out or make a fool of myself. I'm dressed and ready for my graduation ceremony. Everyone is here taking pictures and joking, mom, my stepfather, brother, and my grandmother. Terry, Sr., flew in for my special occasion. Terry was not blood family however, he has been with our family through the good and bad times. He is my grandmother's deceased husbands brother. I'm so happy to have him in my life. Terry, Sr., surprised me with an one-carat diamond necklace with matching ear`rings. They are so beautiful. I just love them, and I can't wait to wear them tonight with my cap and gown. My grandmother, surprised me with an envelop which had five crisp hundred dollar bills inside.

This was more money than I'd seen in my entire life. I was all smiles. Mom and my stepfather were planning this big graduation party for me. Before we left for the graduation ceremony I got another big surprise. Mom handed me a set of keys and told me to look out the window. In the drive way sat a red new corvette with a big ribbon tied on the roof and a sign which read, "Congratulations to the graduate. We are so proud of you." I jumped up and down, screaming, "Oh' my God, Oh' my God!" Everyone was laughing at me, but I didn't care. This had to be the happiest day of my life. Tears started rolling down my face. My stepfather took me in his arms and hugged me. "Stop that before you make your mom and grandmother start crying and they don't look pretty when they cry." Mom picked up something and threw it at him. He ducked and it missed him. We all started laughing. We were all just standing and staring out the window when my brother grabbed the keys out of my hand and started running toward my new car. He had been so quiet, I had forgotten he was even in the room. I was in shock for a few minutes, then I took off chasing him. Everyone followed. I caught him and took the keys from him. Then I opened the driver's side and sit down. The whole family circled around the car smiling. My brother started yelling, "Look out neighbors, get off the road if you don't want to die, Hope is coming." We all laughed. I couldn't drive it yet, because I didn't have a license. But it was still mine. My stepfather reminded us it was time to go. We had a graduation to attend, and we don't want to be late.

Mom, my stepfather and I headed to the graduation. Terry, Sr., and my grandmother followed in his new blue B.M.W. This car brought back memories for my grandmother. This car was just like the car that her husband David had purchased for her many years ago.

The drive to the high school was just a big party for us. We laughed, we sang and just clowned around. We laughed until we almost cried. I've never seen mom and my stepfather acting so silly. It was like something or someone had taken over their bodies and they had no control. Even my brother and I were having the time of our lives. I truly never wanted this evening to come to an end. I had no idea the events of tonight would change my life so drastically. My stepfather instructed us to quiet down, and we did. We wondered what could be wrong. The car slowed down to a crawl. We all started looking around to see what was happening. Off to the left side of the road were several police cruisers. People stopping to look almost caused another accident. The police officer got out of his cruiser to direct traffic around the accident. We found out a drunk driver had hit a pedestrian. The drunk driver was in the back of the police cruiser. There was a body lying on the ground, under a white sheet. You could hear sirens coming from all directions. I didn't want to think about what was happening, because I was focused on getting to the graduation on time. I was thankful my stepfather had forced us to leave a little earlier or we wouldn't have made it to the graduation on time. Traffic was moving slowly. But, we still had plenty of time. Yet, I was silently thinking, if only the traffic would move just a little faster. We continued the ride in silence. I started praying a selfish prayer, "God please make this go away quickly". How could I have known this accident would change my life and my future. The traffic did begin to move and we made it to the graduation with 15 minutes to spare.

Everyone looked so good in their caps and gowns. The smiles on our faces were from ear to ear. The graduates lined up and the music started. This was our signal to take our places. I was so nervous, yet excited to be giving the valedictorian speech on behalf of the graduating class. As the graduating seniors processed I started looking for my boyfriend. I didn't see him anywhere. I thought to myself, "maybe he's just running late and he will slide into line before the ceremony starts". He's always late for class. He's even late for our lunch dates. and for church. So I tried not to worry. I refocused my thoughts on the events at hand. We took our seats, then stood to sing our school's Alma Mater. It was hard knowing that this would the last time we would sing this song. We recited the pledge of allegiance to the flag Again, I searched the end of the line to see if my boyfriend had arrived. He still wasn't here! Things were moving rather fast. We bowed our heads and the class president said a prayer. Next, the superintendant of the school stood and took the podium to say a few words to the graduates. I was next on the program to give my speech. I spoke from my heart. I told them, "That life is not always fair, but it's still good. That we all have a promising future ahead of us if we just work hard". As I was speaking A police officer approached the superintendant and the principal. He whispered in their ears. The look on their faces was one of shock and disbelief. This broke my concentration but, I refocused and continued on. Then I took my seat upon receiving a standing round of applause. I felt good that I had made mom and my stepfather proud of me. The graduating class was asked to stand on their feet to receive their diplomas. A loud noise erupted from the graduating students. This was the moment we all had been waiting for. As each student walked to the podium to receive their diploma my mind reflected back on the police officer and why he was here. What did he say to the superintendent? I also had time to reflect on the fact that someone important in my life was not present. Something had to be terribly wrong for my Bruce to miss his graduation. In my wildest nightmares, I couldn't have envisioned what was to be revealed at the close of the ceremony. My name was being called which brought me back to reality. As I stood in slow motion to walk to the podium to receive my diploma I could hear my family shouting out my name. The superintendant shook my hand and presented me with my diploma. I felt excited, yet sad that my best friend, my boyfriend was not here to share in this special moment. Where was he? Why wasn't he here with me? At that very moment, I realized just how much he meant to me. I was in love for the first time in my life. A sudden eruption of noise caught my attention. The superintendant requested the graduating class to stand to their feet. "With the power vested in me I present to you the Paul Lawrence Dunbar high school graduates. Please move your tassel to the left. Please continue to stand on your feet for a few important words from your principal. A silence fell over the room as the principal walked to the podium with his head bowed down. He cleared his throat, "It is with a sad and heavy heart that I must inform you of the passing of one of your classmates". Even before he said the name I felt light headed and sick to my stomach. "I thought to myself, why didn't I call to check on Bruce"? I prayed silently that it wouldn't be Bruce. The principal asked that we pray for the family of Bruce White. The name was ringing in my ears. My knees felt weak and I fell to the floor screaming, "No, No, it can't be true. This must be a mistake". The room was spinning. All I could see were shoes and feet. I could hear other students crying and sobbing out loud. Suddenly, I recognized the face in front of me, it was my stepfather. He wanted to know if I was okay? I didn't answer, so he just picked me up in his arms and carried me to the car. Again, I heard voices all around me, but I couldn't make out what they were saying or who they were. I really didn't care! I just wanted to go home to the comfort of my room. I just wanted to be left alone with my memories. I needed to process what I've just heard. The ride home was long and painful. I couldn't stop thinking about Bruce. I kept hearing over and over again; "Pray for the White family in the loss of their son, Bruce." How could he be dead on one of the most exciting day of our lives? How could someone so young, sweet, and innocent be dead? I just couldn't imagine my life without him. When we arrived home, the front and back yard, were lit up with balloons and decorations. I stood and glared at the lights for a brief moment before I ran to my room sobbing. I thought, "How could this be happening to me?" Could this just be a terrible nightmare and when I awake things will be different. I cried myself to sleep and I dreamt about Bruce. In my dreams things were very different. I was happy and Bruce was with me. I didn't want to wake up and face the reality that Bruce would no longer be apart of my life. Three days later we buried my best friend, my boyfriend and the love of my life. It was a beautiful homegoing service. Yet, I fear life for me will never be the same.

Chapter Six
Hope's Pain And Despair

SIX

This was supposed to be my freshman year of college. However, I couldn't bring myself to enroll. I had all these emotions I didn't understand. I was sad all the time. I was mad at the world and God. The world no longer looked bright and sunny. I no longer believed that God is a good God and that He protects us. Because if He does where was He when Bruce needed him. Why had God allowed this to happen to me? Why did he allow a drunk driver to kill Bruce? He had such a bright and promising future. Bruce loved me and he told me so. But, I never got a chance to tell him I loved him too. Why God, Why?

I just wanted to sleep my life away. I had nothing to live for. It's been a whole year and the pain is still so great, that it feels like it happen only yesterday. Nobody seems to know how much I'm hurting. I know this sounds strange but my heart hurts. It's like someone put a knife in my heart, and nothing seems to take the pain away. I can't stop thinking about Bruce. I can't sleep and I don't want to eat. Life for me has become a living hell. I want to lock my door and never come out again. Everyone keeps telling me things will get better. But what do they know? Nothing! They have not walked in my shoes. They can't feel my pain, it hurts so bad. I feel so empty inside, and nothing seems to numb the pain. I'm hurting and no one seems to care or to understand. Everyone is going on with their lives as if nothing has happened. I can't. I won't let Bruce's memory die. Everything I look at reminds me of him. No one has ever made me laugh or smile like he did. I'm sure I'll never laugh or feel again the way he made me feel. God why? Why did you allow this to happen? What did I do to deserve this? I thought You were a loving. You took from me the only person who loved and understood me.

Mom and my stepfather have tried to make me go to counseling but I can't, I won't go. Mom has asked her Pastor, Rev. Davis, to come talk with me. I don't want to hear anything he has to say. Unless he can raise the dead, or tell me why God is punishing me and allowed this to happen. My grandmother has cried and prayed with me everyday but not even her love for me has changed anything. I still don't want to live. The thought of leaving this earth seems inviting to me. No more pain or tears. No more decisions to make. I will be with my boyfriend again, forever. I still love him and I miss him so much. My grandmother is worried and distraught. In an act of desperation she called her best friend Terry, Sr., My grandmother knew something needed to change. If things didn't change I wouldn't survive another year like this. I was oblivious to how my state of mind was destroying my family. My brother needed me, he was suffering because, I had abandoned him. Mom and my stepfather's marriage was at the point of divorce because of me. I was blinded by my pain and couldn't and didn't want to see the damage I was causing. I lost my best friend and nothing else mattered to me. I felt helpless and alone.

Terry, Sr., arrived the next day. I wondered why he was here, and who called him. Then, I realized it had to be my grandmother. I didn't want to see him, I knew I would get a lecture from him. Why can't everyone just leave me alone? This is my life and no one can tell me how to live it or what to do.

I hadn't seen Terry, Sr., since my graduation and that terrible night that had changed my life forever. Terry, Sr., came to my room and knocked softly on my bedroom door. "Hope it's Terry, Sr., can I come in?" Before I could reply, he opened the door and let himself in. He hugged me and I cried in his arms like a baby. He cried too as he loved me and felt my pain. He talked and prayed with me for hours. He even managed to make me smile a few times. He pointed out a few things I hadn't thought about. He was the only one brave enough to tell me I was being selfish. At first I got mad and my feelings were hurt. I cried because I didn't understand how he could say something so cruel. Then he explained to me how my grieving wouldn't bring Bruce back. He also said, Bruce wouldn't want me to be so unhappy. That I could honor his memory better by accomplishing what we dreamed of doing together.

Terry, Sr., explained that, "Grief is like an unwelcome visitor. The longer you allow grief to stay the more it will damage, destroy you and everyone around you." How long you grieve doesn't represent how much you loved him. I stopped crying and started listening. What he was saying made so much sense. I also found out that my depression was destroying my brother's life. My brother needed me to help him deal with typical teenage problems. He was no longer a honor student. He was no longer playing sports or even trying to pass his required classes. Because he loved me apart of him died when I decided to give up on life. This time I cried tears but not for myself. I cried for all the damage I had done to my family. After talking with him I realized what I had done by pushing everyone that cared about me out of my life. I kissed and hugged him for caring enough to be honest with me. Knowing my feelings would be hurt, but he told me what I needed to hear. He loved me and for that I was grateful.

He received an emergency phone call and had to cut his visit short. However, his job here was done. We walked to the front door holding hands with a smile on my face. He apologized to the family for having to leave so abruptly, but he promised to return soon. My stepfather took him to the airport. We stood in the doorway and waved goodbye, until the car was out of sight. Then we all joined in a group hug and cried tears of joy. I was back among the living and it felt good to laugh and to be hugged by my family. I loved them so much. I had missed our family gatherings and the closeness we once shared. It's hard to believe that time had passed so quickly. I feel like I have been in a comma for the past year. I let my whole life slip away for an entire year. I have so much to catch up on, where do I start? My first priority had to be my brother.

I had promised Terry, Sr., before he left that I would get grief counseling from my Pastor. I also promised to enroll in college and to get my degree as a Mental Health Counselor. I'm sure it won't be easy, but yet necessary, if I am to help other troubled youth. Even though I had felt all alone in my crisis I wasn't. I realized there are so many teenagers coping and dealing with so many emotional issues. They are feeling helpless with no one to turn to. If I can help just one teenager from traveling down the road I've traveled, then my breakdown will not be in vain.

I'm happy now and I've learned a few valuable lessons that have helped me become who I am today. I know God is real, and no matter what you're going through, pray your way through. Don't give up on life and don't give up on God. You just have to hold on and things will work out in your favor. I have rededicated my life to God. I joined my grandmother's church. I am very active with the youth ministry. My grandmother is an associate minister at the church. Mom, my stepfather and my brother are also very active in the church. We enjoy working together as a family. I have enrolled in college and I'm looking forward to the challenges that lay ahead. I have not been in a serious relationship since

Bruce's death. However, I have met a young man at the church. Greg is active in the youth ministry, and we are sp ending a lot of time together. I like him and he has asked me to go on a date. But, I'm not sure if I'm ready to take that step. The dating scene is still a little scary for me. However, I'm sure that if he is patient things will advance to the next level.

Greg pursued me until I gave into his wishes. After one year of dating, he asked my stepfather, for my hand in marriage. My stepfather, said, "Yes"! We are engaged to be married next year. My grandmother will perform the ceremony. We will be married in the same church where mom, my stepfather and my grandmother recited their wedding vows, surrounded by family and friends. Mom and my stepfather are renewing their wedding vows. They are acting like two teenager in love again. Mom has decided to retire, from her job as a dispatcher. Her job has become very stressful. She wants to retire and do some traveling. My stepfather has decided to work one more year then he too will retire from law enforcement, after thirty-two years of service.

My grandmother's life has been good. She has been happy helping us to mature into God-fearing young adults. My grandmother has been responsible for helping many youth at church turn their lives around. She has only one regret and that is she was never able to open another shelter for the homeless. She wasn't able to because of the memories associated with the shelter. My grandmother never got over losing her first and only love, David. She has not been in a serious relationship since David's death.

She has dated and had many proposals, but she still has too much love in her heart for deceasd husband to allow anyone else into that special place. No one has been worthy to step into that special place in her heart that her husband occupied. After all these years at night my grandmother still dreamt of her late husband and the life they shared. My grandmother is content to live with her memories. She has the love of family, friends, God and that is enough or so she thought.

Chapter Seven
Daniel Jr's Troubles

SEVEN

My brother was indeed having a rough time in school. He was failing every subject. He had been placed on academic probation. Because I was in such a dark place, I hadn't noticed or taken the time to see the changes that had occurred in my brother or my family. I felt so bad that I had neglected everything and everyone. Looking at my brother for the first time in over a year, I could see that he'd loss weight. His eyes were no longer bright and shinny. I could see that he was in pain, and emotionally hurting. I had loss the love of my life and emotionally retreated from life. This took a toll on me, but, I never expected it to have such a devastating effect on my brother's life. I just couldn't figure out what had or was happening in my brother's life that would cause him to give up on life and on God. The only way I was going to find an answer was to talk to him. He alone held the key to the answers I needed. I said a prayer hoping that God would again hear me and listen not for myself but for my brother. I asked God to forgive me and to give me another chance. I prayed that God would give me the right words to say to my brother to relieve his pain.

I knocked on his bedroom door. He yelled out, "Go away, I don't want to talk to anybody." I yelled back, "Daniel it's me, your sister. "I don't have a sister, so go away", I hate you. "You abandoned me when I needed you, so go away. I have nothing to say to you". I called him by his full name, "Daniel Washington, Jr., if you don't open this door you're going to be in big trouble. Now you open this door right now". The room was silent, then I heard his footsteps and the door opening. I entered the room slowly. My brother was sitting on the side of his bed. I wanted to grab him and to hug him, To tell him how much I loved and missed him. I needed him to know that I was sorry for abandoning him. But, I could tell by the way he was sitting with his arms folded across his chest that he was angry with me. Touching and hugging him wasn't a good idea right now. He was full of anger and disdain. I can't say I blamed him. What he said was true. I had abandoned him. The death of a loved one was something I had never experienced before. No one can prepares you for the emotional roller coaster you're on. Everyone deals with grief in their own way and on their own time schedule. Terry, Sr., was my lifesaver. If it hadn't been for him, I would still be in a dark place or maybe even dead

I pleaded, "I do love you. Please let me help you". He shouted back at me, "You don't care and you can't help me, no one can". Then he broke down in tears which almost broke my heart. Because, I can remember saying those same words. As I wiped tears from my eyes, "How do you know I can't help you? If you won't tell me what's wrong, then I can't help you". I could see by the expression on his face he was thinking about the words I had spoken. He cried some more tears, "I told you, no one can help me and I don't want your help. Now, get out!" "My feelings were hurt and I started to leave. Then, I heard this small voice inside my head say, "No, you can't leave, he needs your help even if he thinks he doesn't". So I sat back down on the bed and I told him, No, I'm not leaving until you tell me what's wrong. I'll be here if it takes all night, then I'll be sitting here. I have no place to go and nothing to do". My brother was silent and cried a few more tears. "I'll tell you what's wrong if you will go away and leave me alone. You'll see there's really nothing you can do." Again, there was silence. Before he could share his problem with me there was a knock at the door, it was mom. She opened the bedroom door and without looking at us, she asked, "Is everything alright in here?" Before we could reply she said, "I know you must be hungry and I wanted to let you know dinner is ready. Your father and I would like for you two to come and eat dinner with us". Before she could say another word, in unison we replied, we're not hungry". Mom looked sad but, she closed the door and left us alone. I felt we were making progress. I felt I was close to finding out what was troubling him, but no such luck. My brother looked at me "I'm tired and I need to get some sleep, can we talk about this in the morning?" I wanted to say no let's get to the bottom of this. But, I heard this timid voice saying out loud, "Okay I'm tired too. We can finish this in the morning. "This time I grabbed him, hugged and kissed him. He didn't hug me back, but he didn't resist my affection". So that meant I had made some progress. I left my brother's room with the understanding I would be back bright and early in the morning to finish this discussion. He didn't reply, so I just smiled at him and left his room. I wanted to go back to my bedroom, but, I didn't. Instead, I found myself heading to the living room. Mom and my stepfather were in the dinning room having dinner. They looked surprised to see me take a seat at the table. I really wasn't hungry, but I ate a piece of cake because I knew it would make them happy. We shared small talk as I ate some cake. Then, I excused myself from the table letting them know I was tired and needed some rest. I knew tomorrow was going to be a long day. They agreed and said, "Good night, see you in the morning". I went to bed thinking about my brother. I wondered what could be so wrong in his life that he thought no one could help him. Before I closed my eyes to sleep I said a prayer, asking God to reveal unto me what was troubling my brother and to give me the wisdom I needed to help turn his life around.

I awoke the next morning at the crack of dawn. Not wanting to disturb anyone, I just lay in bed starring at the ceiling wondering if this would be a good or bad day. Only time would tell. When I heard running water I knew the family was up and moving. I went down stairs to speak to mom and my stepfather. I grabbed a glass of orange juice and a piece of toast. I said a prayer again. Not for myself but for my brother. I proceeded upstairs to my brother's room. I knocked on the door. Not sure if he was awake or that he would let me in. But, much to my surprise I heard, "Come in"! I opened his bedroom door slowly and walked in. Again, he was sitting on the side of his bed. This time something was different about him. He didn't look so angry and he stood to greet me and gave me a big hug. I was surprised but, so happy at his show of affection. This was indeed progress. I cried on his shoulder as he hugged me. He wiped my tears away, "My sister, no more tears. He let me knnow he didn't mean what he said yesterday. He loved me and he was happy to have me back in his life. He missed me. He asked me to never push him out his life again".

I looked my brother in his eyes and promised never to allow that to happen again. For I had missed him too. With those words spoken I felt like a big weight had been lifted off my shoulders. We just sat for a few moments just smiling and holding hands. I took that moment to say a prayer thanking God for working things out in my favor and for showing us His love and mercy. We had been through so much. I didn't know what to say or where to start. But, I felt I should try to explain why I had to escape from everyone and everything. It was hard for me to put into words what I had been feeling. But if I wanted my brother to open up and pour out his pain to me then I needed to share my pain. He needed to know how much pain and guilt I had been carrying around inside of me for over a year. My dilemma now was how do I put into words what I was feeling. Words that a sixteen year old would understand. All I could think of at that moment was, "Oh' God, Help me. I can't do this without you". Tears started rolling down my face again at the thought of sharing my grief and pain. I didn't want to cry, but I couldn't control myself. I was so sick of crying tears. But my counselor says there's healing power in the tears that I shed. That it's a process I must go through. I looked to the heavens and again, asked God for strength. My brother took me in his arms to comfort me. He said, "Take your time sister, you've been through a lot of pain, so just let it all out. We have no where to go and nothing to do. So if it takes all night, then so be it". Those words brought a smile to my face for a brief moment. He continued, "I'm going to sit right here until you get it all out". With that being said, I took a deep breath and began to share my whole nightmare. My brother held my hand and didn't say a word until I finished talking. Then he took me in his arms again and held me for what seemed like hours. But in fact it had been only five or ten minutes. When my brother released me the next words out of his mouth put a big smile on my face. "I'm so proud of you. Thank you for sharing your story, your pain with me". He knew it was hard. "He loved me for being brave enough to share my deepest thoughts with him". All of a sudden I realized we hadn't eaten since this morning. I'm starving can we take a break and get a bite to eat". He agreed and we went to the kitchen. We made sandwiches and got drinks and took them back to his room. We laughed and reminisced over our youthful years. It felt good to be sharing quality time with my brother the way things use to be. At that very moment, it seemed like we were kids again and didn't have any troubles or worries. I wished we could relive the good old days. Those were the days I felt safe, happy, secure and loved. Oh' to be able to turn back the hands of time. Our trip down memory lane was brought to a sudden halt. We heard my stepfather's voice calling our names. Mom and my stepfather were happy to see us bonding again. I'm sure they had plenty of questions but they respected our privacy. They chose to wait patiently for answers. We laughed because we felt like two kids who had been caught with their hands in the cookie jar. However, that was so far from the truth. We were both grown young adults, dealing with adult problems.

The room went silent again. My brother's whole mood seemed to change. I could once again feel tension in the room. I knew it was time to discuss what was troubling him. We could no longer avoid the subject. However, I didn't know how to tactfully approach the subject, so I didn't. I waited for my brother to express and share what he was feeling.

Chapter Eight
Daniel Jr. Faces His Bully

EIGHT

Finally, my brother took a deep breath and shared with me he hated school. He wanted to dropout however, mom and dad wouldn't hear of it. My stepfather expressed that no child of his was going to be a drop out. He believed, if you wanted to succeed in life you must get a high school diploma and graduate from college. So my brother gets up every morning. He goes to class and after attendance is taken he skips out. He hates his teachers, classmates and everything associated with that school. Not having you there to talk to even made things worse. Mom and dad just don't understand what it's like being a teenager in school these days. They are still living in the dinosaur age. So it's impossible to talk to them about my problems. Nobody, not even our grandmother, understands what it's like for me. Things had gotten so bad he just wanted to slit his wrist but he didn't have the nerve to follow through with his plan. I was shocked to hear that he was in so much pain that he would rather leave this earth than face his problems. I just couldn't image what could be that bad. I didn't interrupt him even though I wanted to scream out what's wrong. I just sat quietly waiting for him to let it all out. My heart was breaking knowing he was in such pain and felt so helpless to do anything about it. My brother had been talking a whole hour and I still didn't know what was troubling him and making his life so unbearable. My brother abruptly stopped talking and burst into tears. We were making such progress his sudden show of emotions had caught me by surprise. But now it was my time to be the big sister, my time to comfort him. I took him in my arms and hugged him tightly until the tears stopped flowing. He took another deep breath and started all over again. This was draining me emotionally, but it was necessary. I wanted to do all that I could to help my brother find peace and happiness. I didn't know how I was going to do it. All I knew was that my brother needed help. I would do anything to put a smile on his face and help to turn his life around. My brother was just too young and to smart to throw his life away. My brother talked for another hour. But I still had no idea what was bothering him. He was just repeating himself over and over again. I didn't want to be rude and to interrupt him, but I just didn't understand his crisis. He was talking a mile a minute, but I wasn't understanding the dilemma. Finally, I did interrupt my him. Can you be a little more specific. Tell me when your trouble first started and who or what started the problem. My brother stopped talking and just stared at me as if he could see straight through me. He stood to his feet as if he was sleep walking and he didn't say a word. I didn't know if I had said something wrong or if I had hurt his feeling. For a moment, I regretted opening my big mouth.

Then my brother said the first thing that made sense to me. It all started his freshman year of high school. Wanting so bad to be popular and liked by all his peers but regrettably that wasn't the case. No matter how hard he tried he didn't fit in. They made fun of the way he looked and the way he dressed. Everything he did was funny to them. They talked about him behind his back and sometimes to his face. Before the year was up they started playing cruel jokes on him. One of the seniors at the high school who hated him for no apparent reason. He thought it would be funny to put trash in his locker. My brother was so embarrassed when he opened his locker. The trash fell to the floor and everyone started laughing at him. When he told his teachers they said it was a harmless prank and he should not take it so seriously. That's the reason he hated his teachers and the students. Now, someone was spreading rumor that he was gay just because he was not dating anyone. They had tried to set him up with some girl. When he refused her advances she joined in on spreading the rumor. He was being bullied on his phone and on his social network and nobody seemed to care. If things weren't bad enough a big football player was taking his lunch money. The bully promised he would kick his butt if he didn't get the money daily. If he saw him in the hallway the bully would take pleasure in knocking him to the floor. If not the floor into the school lockers. The bully was happy when he could humiliate my brother or cause him great pain. The school takes a blind eye to what the bully was doing because he's a football player. When my brother thought things couldn't get worse they did. The bully caught him in the bathroom and pushed his face into the toilet and dared my brother to tell anyone. If my brother told anyone, the bully threatened to burn down our house. My brother didn't tell for fear of retaliation. My brother couldn't stand the thought of his family being hurt because of something he did or didn't do, so he suffered in silence.

Two of my brother's friends committed suicide because they were being bullied. They too tried to talk to their teachers, parents, and counselors, but it did no good. My brother felt "that suicide looked like an escape to him because he couldn't take the pain anymore". He felt if he died tomorrow, no one would miss him and no one would care. What was he supposed to do when no one would listen or cared about the pain he was living with daily. My brother believed if you're not one of the rich kids or a sports hero, no one cared about your feelings or what was happening in your life. He couldn't find any peace not even when he closed his eyes at night. He would have this reoccurring nightmare that he was back at school and this time he was being tortured and the teachers, the principal joined in on the fun. His nights were as bad as his days. He wished he didn't have to go school or to sleep ever again. My brother wished he could blow up the building with the students and staff inside. He felt they deserved to be punished for all the pain he had suffered along with hundreds of other students. My brothers situation was critical and something had to be done before he acted on his feelings. Which would only make matters worst.

Now, that I had a clearer understanding of what was happening, I was more determined than ever to find a solution and to put an end to the bullying being done to my brother and other helpless victims.

Chapter Nine
Sweet Revenge

NINE

Once the whole situation was revealed, I felt really helpless too. I didn't know what to say or what to tell him to do. I was totally in the dark and didn't have a clue about this type of behavior. However, I had to do something. This didn't happen when I was in school. If it did, it never happened to me. I sat on the edge of the bed in shock. I never could have imagined this happening in the school I graduated from. Or that it was happening to someone I loved. I broke my silence and asked my brother, "Have you told mom and dad what is happening to you." He hung his head down, "No, I'm too frightened and embarrassed to tell them." I didn't say a word. I was so mad that my brother had to endure this bullying and that no one had done anything to stop it. I'm sure my brother wasn't the only one being tormented.

The administration had chosen to look the other way. Because the bully was a member of the football team, and they believed he could do no wrong. After much thought I told my brother the first thing we must do is to tell mom and dad. They really need to know what is happening to you. My brother sobbed, "no, no, they can't find out what's been happening." Because, they would only fuss at him for not telling them sooner.

My brother felt they would be disappointed and hurt that he didn't turn to them in his hour of need. My brother was also afraid of losing their love and respect. My brother looked me in my eyes and pleaded, "Please don't tell them, it was hard enough telling you." He just couldn't bear repeating his story to another living soul. He felt he would die from the embarrassment. I thought about not telling them for a brief moment. Then, I realized my brother was wrong. Mom and my stepfather loved him and nothing would change that. As I sat on the side of the bed thinking about what my brother was going through because of one individual, I got mad all over again. As I pondered what to do an idea came to my mind. Yes, mom and my stepfather had to be told. But only after we put our heads together and gave the bully a taste of his own medicine. A wicked smile came across my face. My brother was trying to read the facial expression on my face. But I knew he couldn't in his wildest dreams comprehend what I was thinking. So I shared my plan with him. I was sure there would be consequences for our actions but the punishment would be worth it. My brother would have to be a man and accept responsibility for his actions. My brother had a smile on his face as I explained my plan of action. This was the first time I'd seen him smile since I entered his room. I had to repeat the plan several times. I also had to work on building my brother's self confidence. He loved my idea, but he wasn't sure that he could pull it off. He paced the floor trying to convince himself that he could carry out my plan of action. We were once again interrupted. This time it was our grandmother. She wanted to see with her own eyes the transformation that had taken place in both her grandchildren. She yelled upstairs, "Come down here. Don't make an old woman climb those steps". We laughed, then we ran down the steps and planted a kiss on both her checks. "Now this is what I prayed to see before I died". We both yelled out, "You can't die before you're very, very old and maybe, now even then". My grandmother laughed and threw a shoe at us. Mom and my stepfather entered the living room and asked us, "What's going on in here?" Our laughter could be heard outside. We explained what had been said, then we all erupted in laughter.

Mom fixed a quick chicken casserole and we all dined together just like the old days. Mom's great cooking brought back such pleasant memories. We all ate as if this would be our last meal. My grandmother gave the blessing. She thanked God for blessing this family and restoring peace unto us. My grandmother got quiet for a moment, "I don't know what miracle has taken place in this family, but I thank God for the laughter and the joy. It's been a long time coming". What my grandmother didn't know was that we still had a big battle ahead of us. But for now we would just focus on the present.

We all hugged, kissed and went our separate ways. My grandmother went home to her little cottage. Mom and my stepfather went to their bedroom. My brother and I went back to his bedroom to rehearse his starring role in tomorrow's revenge skit. Again, I needed to reassure him that he could do what was needed and he would feel much better when he finished. If things went as planned he would also have control of his life again. He would have a few cuts and bruises but nobody at that school would ever bother him again.

My brother had missed school for several days. However, this day he was up early dressing. He was eager to get there this day. There was no fear in his heart. It was time to take a stand against bullying. No one would ever hit him again or attempt to take anything from him after this. This day would be different from all the other days at school. When he got off the bus with his athletic bag in his hand who was the first person to greet him except the high school bully, Eric. My brother held his head up and continued walking straight ahead. Until he heard a voice that said, "Hey punk, where's my lunch money?" My brother replied, "Leave me alone, it's my lunch money, and you can't have it." My brother heard laughter, then he felt hands pulling on his clothes. My bother warned him again, "Leave me alone. You have no right to take anything from me or any other student in this building." Again, my brother heard laughter and felt hands trying to push him to the floor. My brother resisted and this made the bully mad. Eric hadn't noticed that my brother was carrying an athletic bag until my brother reached down to open it. He took a big stick out of the bag and softly said, "I told you to leave me alone." Then my brother proceed to attack the bully. He hit him several times. Eric fell to the floor screaming. Are you crazy, do you know who I am? My brother replied, "Yes, a bully who's going to get his butt whipped if he doesn't leave me alone." He then, shouted, "Do you understand me? The youngman on the floor held up his hands as to surrender, "Okay, Okay, man, I won't bother you again, I promise." The students standing in the hallway erupted into laughter. This time the laughter was not at my brother's expense. For once it felt good not to be on the receiving end of the bad joke. Upon hearing all the commotion, the principal stepped into the hallway. He inquired, "What's going on here? Everybody get to class or I'll write detention slips for everyone of you." Students started to scatter like roaches. The hallway was cleared in a matter of seconds. After the crowd cleared the hallway, the principal noticed the Eric on the floor. The principal questioned Eric as to what had happened, and why was he on the floor. The principal extended his hand to help the Eric up on his feet. Then, he recognized the school's star football player. After much thought Eric stated, my brother had pushed him down and hit me with a big stick. He said, "He hadn't done anything to provoke my brother. The principal questioned, "Are you alright, if so you may return to your classroom." I will get to the bottom of this. The principal called over the PA system for Daniel Washington, Jr., to come to his office. My brother was surprised to hear his name being called because, this had never happened before. My brother exited his room and went directly to the principal's office. The principal told my brother to take a seat. He didn't give my brother an opportunity to explain his side of the story. The principal just instructed his secretary to contact Daniel Washington's parent's and that he would be going home for 10 days. He also instructed her to pull the necessary paper to have my brother suspended and maybe even expelled. My brother took out his cell phone and called me. With pride in his voice he whispered, "Your plan worked". My brother did just what I told him to do and it had worked. You should have seen that bully laying on the floor, begging me to stop. But the school is calling mom and dad please come with them to help me explain what has happened. He really didn't care what they did to him. He was happy knowing that the old bully wouldn't mess with him again. My brother was sent to his locker to get his personal belongings. As he walked through the hallway he felt different. He felt stronger and happier than he had felt in a long time. Students in the hallway who never spoke to him, were speaking now. Some even seemed to approve of his actions. Some students gave him high-fives, saying, "You go boy, good job". Some of the girls hugged and kissed him on his cheek. He heard several students discussing what had just happened. He felt good. He was probably going to be suspended for ten days, but that didn't matter. The only thing that mattered was that he had gained the respect of his peers, and he had his confidence back. We arrived within the hour. Mom and my stepfather were surprised to be receiving a call from the school. This was the first time since my brother had enrolled in school that they had received a call from the principal's office. They couldn't imagine what could be wrong. Mom was afraid my brother had been injured or was sick. We entered the principal's office to see my brother sitting in a chair smiling as if nothing was wrong. "Mother instructed my brother to take that grin off his face. You better have a good reason for being in this office. Are you sick? He replied, "No, ma'am." His reply only made mom madder."

The principal informed them that my brother was being suspended. My stepfather calmly questioned, "Why and what had he done?" The principal never looked up. He just replied, "Fighting." My stepfather shook his head, "That's doesn't sound like my son. "Who was he fighting and what were they fighting about?" My stepfather was cut off. "That's not important. We have a school policy no fighting and no exceptions." My stepfather didn't like his attitude nor his tone of voice. He questioned, the principal had he talked to my brother about what happened." The principal answered, "No, he didn't need to. He had seen for himself what was done". "He had to pick their star football player up off the floor. That's all he needed to see." Now, there's nothing else to discuss. Will you leave my office and take your son with you?" My stepfather was so mad, I believe I could see the steam coming from his ears. "My mother in a timid voice suggested we leave.." But before my stepfather left the principal's office he informed him that he was going to get to the bottom of this. When he did he would see him at the Board of Education meeting, and then in the courtroom. "My son has rights and he believed his son's rights had been violated. If that was the case, you'll be paying for my son's next four years of college. He bet that would change his attitude." With that being said, my stepfather turned to leave with the family close on his heels. I tried to tell my stepfather it was my fault but, he wanted to hear the facts from my brother.

The ride home was stressful. My stepfather did all the talking, but he was holding a conversation with himself. I've never seen my stepfather so upset. He repeated over and over, "I'll show him, who does he think he's dealing with. He hasn't seen the last of me. I'm gonna see that his job is taken. You can't treat people like trash and get away with it." My stepfather fussed all the way home. When we got inside he questioned my brother. "Son we need to talk."My stepfather was still upset. But I believed that when he heard my brother's side of the story, he would be proud of him. My brother took a seat and began to explain what had been happening for the past few years. Now, my stepfather understood why my brother had been coming home with cuts and bruises all over his body. My stepfather looked like he wanted to cry, but of course, he didn't. Because, he believed that real men don't cry. After hearing my brother's side of the story my stepfather got mad all over again. He called the principal's office but, the secretary answered. "The princpial is not in his office." My stepfather knew the principal was avoiding his call. He went to the board meeting seeking justice, however, they wouldn't let him address the situation. My stepfather hired a lawyer to represent my brother's case against the school board and the principal.

Chapter Ten
A Visit To The White House

TEN

The attorney appealed my brother's suspension and filed a lawsuit on his behalf. He also wrote a letter to the White House Administration and President Obama. Because of the letter, my stepfather received a letter from the public relations department at the White House. We were invited to the White House to discuss a "Stop-Bullying Campaign" with the President and Mrs. Obama. Included in the letter were first class tickets for the entire family. The family was so excited to be going to the White House. We were scheduled to leave on Wednesday evening. Hotel reservations had been made for us. We were to meet with the President and First Lady Obama on Thursday afternoon. The entire family arrived at the White House one hour before the scheduled meeting. It would take that long to get through security. We were ushered to the west wing conference room. The room was full of teachers, students, administrators and parents. We were all there for a common goal to put an end to bullying. The President and First Lady Obama entered the room. We all stood staring in disbelief that we were in the White House looking into the face of the President. The President was introduced by one of the White House officials. President Obama took the podium, he smiled, "Hello and welcome to the White House. We are here because we can take steps to prevent bullying. Today marks the debut of a website titled, "Stopbullying.gov" this is a site that provides information from various government agencies on how kids, teens, young adults and others in the community can prevent or stop bullying." Once the President finished, First Lady Obama took the podium, "We as parents need to make a real effort to be engaged in our children's lives, to listen to them and be there for them when they need us. Mrs. Obama informed us that 43% of kids say they have been bullied verbally and online. 80% of teenagers today use a cell phone, thus it is the most common medium for cyber bullying. Victims of cyber bullying are two to nine times more likely to consider committing suicide. Studies have found that 75% of students have visited a website to bash another student. Parents you should know that 68% of teens today believe that cyber bullying is a serious problem. It was so quiet you could hear a pin drop. Once the Obama's finished speaking they asked us to stand and share briefly our experience with bullying. Mrs. Obama wanted to know, "What we thought could be done to prevent bullying?" My stepfather, whispered in my brother's ear, "Son get up and share your story with the President and First Lady Obama." My brother looked at his dad as if he just told him to go play in traffic. Fear gripped my brother's whole body, but he stood to his feet and raised his hand. The President saw his hand, "Young man what's your name? My brother, proudly stated, "Daniel Washington Jr.," Then the President inquired "Daniel Washington do you have a story you would like to share with us? My brother shook his head yes, and shared his story with everyone in the room. He shared what a nightmare high school had been for him and what could have been done to prevent the bullying. When he finished he was given a standing round of applause. But, the next thing that happened almost caused his knee's to buckle. The President and First Lady Obama left the podium to shake his hand. First Lady Obama even gave him a hug. At that moment I thought my brother might pass out, but he didn't. He just stood their as if his feet were glued to the floor. The family stood on our feet looking like a deer caught in the headlights. This had to be the most exciting day of our lives.

The conference was coming to a close. There was one thing left to do. President Obama was to sign a law against bullying. We all stood around watching. The President turned to my brother, "Daniel you shared your story with everyone so he felt it's only befitting that we name this new law in my brother's honor. We will call it the "Daniel Washington Jr., "Stop Bullying Law." My brother's mouth dropped wide open he couldn't believe what he had heard. I thought for sure that mom and my grandmother were going to faint. I think they would have if my stepfather hadn't stepped in to give them support.

As for me and my stepfather we had this silly grin plastered on our faces. We couldn't stop smiling. My little brother had a state law with his name on it. Wow!

The final event of the evening was a banquet in honor of the new "Daniel Washington Jr., Stop Bullying Law". The food looked delicious, but we weren't hungry. I think we weren't hungry because of all the excitement over the events of the day. I couldn't believe we had spent all day at the White House.

The day was coming to a close, but I didn't want to leave. The White House was so beautiful. Pictures just don't do it justice. I learned that the White House is located at 1600 Pennsylvania Avenue. The White House has 132 rooms, with 32 bathrooms, and 16 levels to accommodate all the people who lived in, worked in and visited the white house. I couldn't help but reflect on the famous people who had walked these hallways. I was standing in the same room where John F. Kennedy and Martin L. King had once stood. Looking at all the pictures of past and present presidents really made me stand in awe. This was a history lesson that we would never forget.

Finally, it was time to return to the hotel to start packing for the return flight home. Our flight home would depart early in the morning. The flight home was ong, but uneventful. When we arrived at the airport we were surprised to find news reporters waiting on us, with cameras rolling. They were treating us as if we were famous celebrities, yelling and screaming questions at us. "Did you like President Obama and his wife? Why did you go to the White House?" My stepfather yelled at us, "Don't say a word it's none of their business. I thought it was funny, but my stepfather didn't. He warned them to leave us alone or he would get a restraining order from the courts and he was serious. I just didn't think that it was that serious. However, I kept my mouth shut and did as I was told.

Once we were home, things returned to normal. Dishes to be washed, floors to vacuumed and garbage to be taken out. Being in Washington D.C. now seemed like a dream.

Chapter Eleven
Daniel' Jr. Returns To School

ELEVEN

My brother got up bright and early and dressed to return to school. All he wanted was for his life to return to normal. When he returned to school, things still weren't normal. Students pointed their fingers at him and whispered as he walked down the hallway. Even the teachers standing in the hallways were staring at him like he had two heads. Finally, one of the teachers approached him, "Daniel, you need to report to the principal's office." My brother didn't ask any questions. He just went to the office. When he walked through the office the secretary looked at him as if he had just robbed a bank and his face was on a most wanted poster. My brother took a seat outside the principal's office and waited.

He waited a hour, and no one said a word to him. My brother was getting annoyed. Finally, he took out his cell phone and called his father. "Dad, please come get me, something is wrong. I have been sitting in the principal's office for the past hour. I'm tired of this and I'm ready to come home." My stepfather picked him up and went straight to his lawyer's office. The lawyer informed him that the principal was holding an emergency expulsion hearing to remove my brother for the rest of the school year. He also found out that the principal was upset because the football team had lost their game because my brother assaulted their football star and he couldn't play. My brother also injured the young man's hand and arm during the fight. When my stepfather heard their grounds for expulsion he was furious. My brother thought it was funny and he started laughing. However, my stepfather didn't see any humor in the charges. My stepfather wanted to contact the principal's office but, decided against it because he was sure he couldn't remain professional. He decided to let his attorney fight this battle. The attorney filed a rebuttal to the expulsion hearing. He also sued the Board of Education and the principal for failure to provide a safe environment for my brother. The attorney sued for physical and emotional damages inflicted in the amount of one-millon dollars for damages past and present years.

My stepfather wanted to make sure the principal would think twice before he allowed this to happened in his building again. My stepfather sent a follow-up letter to

President Obama and First Lady Michelle informing them of the situation. President Obama in turn wrote a letter to the school board and the principal. "He informed them he was disappointment with their actions. He reminded them of the penalties of not enforcing the new "Daniel Washington Jr. "Stop Bullying State Law." He also informed them that if this matter was not handled swiftly he would be making a personal visit to the city. He warned them that there would be stiff penalties for anyone breaking this law." A copy of the letter was sent to all involved parties and a certified letter was sent to the high school. The principal was upset, but he knew he couldn't win a fight against a state law. Therefore, he ordered his staff and administrators to hold a seminar on the "Daniel Washington Jr. Stop Bullying law." The student body signed a pledge to help enforce the new "Stop Bullying Law". The principal had to educate the student body about the new law and the consequences of breaking the law. "As required by legislation the district policy on bullying and other forms of aggressive behavior must be available in the office of the building principal or building supervisor. A notice must be posted in each building and department."

The family waited patiently for a ruling on my brother's expulsion hearing. It took seven days for the appointed officials to render a verdict. After reviewing all the evidence and hearing testimony from all involved the judge rendered his verdict against the school board and the principal. The judge ruled that immediate action to be taken against the following. The administrators, faculty, athletic department and the football team. Along with students and parents involved in this tragic turn of events . No one would go unpunished who had knowledge that this bulling was occurring.

A task force was formed to interview the entire community. After the panel completed their interviews, the results were turned over to the superintendent. After reviewing the results the superintendent was surprised to find out that other incidents of bullying had been reported. They too had been ignored or lightly dealt with. Many students had been threatened and told not to complain or to tell anyone. If they told their family members would be hurt or maybe even killed. Due to the investigation many students and parents felt more comfortable and came forth to share their stories of abuse.

Chapter Twelve
School Board Found Guilty

TWELVE

Justice was swiftly delivered and heads started to roll. The principal was placed on administrative leave for five days without pay. Several staff members and administrator's were removed from their positions for having first hand knowledge of the bullying and doing nothing. Members of the athletic department received verbal and written reprimands. The entire football team was placed on probation for one year. They had to forfeit all games for the rest of the season. Several students were suspended for contributing to the incident of bulling. Last, but not least, the star football player Eric White, was suspended for ten days and he was also removed from his quarterback position for the duration of the season. These sanctions resulted in his losing his scholarships.

Eric White's family was ordered by the courts to pay 10% of the funds awarded to the Washington family in thirty days. The superintendent wrote a letter of apology to the Washington's and he demanded that the principal of the high school do the same. A letter of apology from the superintendent and the principal was also addressed to my brother The letter stated that all charges had been dropped and that he could return to school first thing on Monday morning. My brother felt justified after reading the humbling letter of apology. The funds received from the lawsuit were placed in a trust fund for my brother The funds would be released to him on his eighteenth birthday.

It had been two weeks since my brother had walked through the doors of the high school. He felt nervous and hesitant about returning to school. But, my stepfather encouraged him to let go of his fears. He assured him that it might not be as bad as he thought. My stepfather, told my brother to step out on faith and believe that God would protect him." He truly believed that if my brother had faith, God would see him through. God had already worked things out in his favor. My brother reluctantly went to school and he soon discovered that his father was right. The students and staff welcomed him back with endearing words and compliments. My brother couldn't believe this was the same school he had left three weeks ago. The student body and staff treated him like he was a V.I.P. He didn't know how to react to the special treatment he was receiving. When my stepfather picked my brother up after school he was so excited he couldn't get the words out. My brother had been asked to be valedictorian of his senior class. What an honor to represent the graduating class of Paul Lawrence Dunbar. My brother had no idea what he would say, but he knew he could count on me to give him a few words of advice. As my stepfather drove slowly home, he just listened to my brother as he went on and on about his day at school. Finally, my brother seemed to be running out of energy and words to say. He sat quietly reflecting on what a big responsibility he was undertaking. He knew he couldn't embarrass himself or the family by saying or doing anything stupid. This would be the high light of his high school years. He also reflected back on my graduation. He remembered how Bruce was hit and killed by a drunk driver and didn't make it to his graduation. He reflected on the pain and sadness that I felt at the passing of my best friend/boyfriend. His untimely death had sent my life spinning out of control. He hoped that his graduation would be different. He only wanted tears of joy and happiness. My brother couldn't wait to get home to share the good news with us. Before my stepfather could turn the engine off my brother jumped out of the car and ran into the house with this big grin on his face. He didn't wait for mom or me to asked him how his day was. He just blurted out school was great today. You will never guess who has been asked to be the valedictorian for the graduating class. Mom smiled and played along. "No, I can't imagine who has been asked."

" well whomever it is, I hope they know what a great

responsibility this is." Mom began to call out the names of who she thought might have been asked to represent the graduating class. When my brother couldn't stand it anymore he yelled out. "It's me, I've been chosen to represent the class, me, me, it's me."Mom laughed at my brother's excitement, and then looked him in his face, with a straight face, "Are you sure you want to take on such a big responsibility?" She knew the answer to the question before the words came out of her mouth. She knew my brother would make a great valedictorian speaker. We were all so proud of my brother. He has such a promising future.

Unfortunately, not everyone was happy about my brother becoming the valedictorian. Just a handful of students objected to my brother being given the honor. They started a petition to hold a recount on the votes which had elected my brother as valedictorian. When they couldn't get the necessary votes they formed a committee and went to the superintendent with their concerns. The superintendent informed them they had a right to object and voice their opinion however, he thought my brother was a good choice. He would consider their choice for valedictorian only if they could acquire the necessary signatures for a recount. The students left the superintendent's office very disappointed that he did not side with them. They whispered among themselves that they thought the superintendent was being bias just because my brother had a "Stop Bullying law" named after him. But, they weren't impressed by the new law. They thought my brother didn't deserve the recognition he was receiving, nor the honor of being the valedictorian. They vowed to get the necessary signatures to remove him as valedicatorian, even if it took the rest of the semester.

My brother went about his daily routine without being affected by the small handful of students who wanted the honor of being valediction taken from him. He dismissed it as jealousy from a few haters.

However, a few of my brother's supporters decided to fight fire with fire. So they too started a campaign for him. His classmates began getting signatures to insure that Daniel, Jr., would remain valedictorian for the graduating class. His supporters believed he had earned the right to represent the graduating class. They also vowed to see that my brother would be the valedictorian speaker. My brother's supporters also went to the superintendent to gain his support. The superintendent was trying so hard to remain neutral however, he was having a difficult time. The superintendent once again stated he would honor the individual, with the most signatures. Although, he secretly wanted my brother to remain valedictorian, because he liked my brother. He belived my brother was a fighter and he didn't drop out when things got rough. He fought back and won, against all odds he came out victorious. My brother's story was unique and special. It's a story that needs to be shared with all graduating students. Each group of supporters worked hard to acquire the necessary signatures, however, it was a tie. The situation was getting out of control.

Students were arguing and threatening to do bodily harm to other students. It was now two days before the graduation and they still had no solution to the problem. My brother felt honored to be selected to be valedictorian, however, he didn't want to be the reason the graduating class was at each others throats. After much thought, he decided to withdraw his name as valedictorian. Surprisingly his decision not to be valedictorian, didn't cause him any stress. However, my brother wasn't sure if this was a good decision so he went to our grandmother, for advice. Upon hearing my brother's dilemma, my grandmother was not pleased with his decision. After much thought, my grandmother had a solution that she thought would make everyone happy. My grandmother suggested that they both speak as the valedictorian for the graduating class. She felt sure this was a compromise everyone would be happy with, and she was right. The graduation went forth with both speakers and was a great success. My brother graduated with honors and is now headed to Ohio State University.

Chapter Thirteen
Destiny Has Breast Cancer

THIRTEEN

The whole family had been under tremendous stress during the year. But, with God's help we managed to overcome each obstacle. Just when I thought life was returning to normal mom went to the doctor to get her yearly check up, a mammogram. Mom had never had an abnormal pap spear or mammogram so she wasn't worried. She had no family history of breast cancer and had never known anyone else who was diagnosed with the disease. However, this time things were different. Mom's lab reports came back as having found a suspicious lesion that neither she nor her doctor could feel. It was discovered in her right breast. Mom took the news rather good. However, the family went into panic mode. Mom was the one comforting us. "No need to get upset now. We have a long battle ahead of us.

But with God all things are possible." She was a child of God and knew He wouldn't let any harm or danger come to His child. Mom then called my grandmother to the house, so that she could offer up a prayer of healing to God. After that everything happened at record speed. Mom's breast surgeon confirmed the diagnosis of breast cancer with a needle biopsy after further imaging with an ultrasound. Shortly afterwards she underwent surgical treatment with a partial right mastectomy and sentinel axillary lymph node dissection. Mom was a trooper. She never once complained or questioned God's will for allowing this to happen. Mom felt she was beautifully broken so that she could minister to others.

On the other hand my brother and I were falling apart. We were mad with God that He allowed this to happened to our mother. Mom didn't deserve this. She was a great person and a wonderful mother. She cooked and ate, heathy meals and demanded that we do the same. My stepfather looked worried throughout mom's heath crisis, but he never voiced a negative opinion or questioned God's will. He prayed and held her hand to comfort her as we waited for the doctor to inform us what the next step was to be. Mom's surgery was performed, and her cancer was identified as a node-negative. Because she was in the early stage of the disease her surgeon ordered an oncotype DX. Some initial lab results had indicated that she would be a candidate for chemotherapy, but the results from oncotype DX suggested that mom would not benefit from chemotherapy. Mom had completed radiation therapy and was now on hormonal treatments with an aromatase-inhibitor. She felt blessed that the cancer was now gone from her body and the pain was too. Mom is no longer fearful of the small things that can happen in life. The cancer scare had made her life all the more precious. Mom didn't share with us her fears until the surgery and the radiation therapy were complete. She later shared with us that the worse part of this illness was the shock of hearing and saying the word cancer. When she heard the word cancer, she felt out of control. The realization of knowing your life could be coming to an end was so terrifying. Facing the probability that she would be leaving this earth. Facing her own demise and leaving everyone and everything she loved behind was in fact the most frightening. The thought of having chemotherapy, being sick and loosing her hair really had her scared to death. She had heard so many horror stories about chemotherapy and the side effects. She was so relieved that she was able to go on with her life without the interruptions of chemotherapy. She thanked God for sparing her life and not having to experience chemotherapy treatments. She thanked God for her skilled Oncologist and the love and support of her family.

I admired how my mother dealt with this whole crisis. She had such a positive and loving spirit. Even though she was in great pain, she never cried or complained in front of us. I guess I did enough crying for the both of us. The hardest part is now over. The doctor has ordered her to rest to allow her body to heal. He has also ordered her to have physical therapy. You would think the doctor's orders would be simple to follow. However, staying in bed and doing nothing was hard for mom. She loved housecleaning and cooking. Mom didn't know the meaning of the word, rest or to stay in bed. Mom led a very busy life and that's the way she liked it. To keep mom in bed, my stepfather hired a housekeeper to clean and cook while mom recuperated. Mom wasn't happy about having a stranger in her house touching her things. Mom refused to allow the housekeeper in her bedroom to clean. This area of the house was private and off limits. my stepfather decided not to argue with her about that fact. If it made her feel better he was willing to do anything. He was just so happy to have her healthy and happy again. Mom's health had returned. She had been released by her doctor to return to her regular activities.

Once she was released she started looking for a cancer survivors group. The only group she found was a hour away from us. She was not happy about having to drive so far. So she attended a few meetings took notes and then decided to form her own support group.. Mom was excited about hosting her first meeting. She wasn't sure if anyone would attend, so she decided to hold the first meeting in our home. Much to her surprise there was standing room only. Many of them lived within blocks of our home. They too hadn't wanted to make the long drive to attend a survivors meeting. Mom was so happy to see each one of the cancer survivors. Each one had such a touching story to share of how cancer had ravished their bodies and how they fought to survive. Upon entering, these women were complete strangers, but before they left they knew each others story. They cried on each others shoulders and bonded because of the pain they had endured. There wasn't a dry eye in the place, including me and my grandmother. We stood in the kitchen out of sight listening and crying over the heartbreaking stories. The survivors group will met the second Saturday of each month. Mom secured a meeting room at the YWCA for all future meetings. She had survived cancer and now it was her mission to support others who are struggling with cancer. She also planned to host and run in the next marathon for cancer survivors. Mom's near death experience had changed her outlook on life. It had given her a new zeal for life. I have heard her repeat over and over again, at her meeting, "Don't put off until tomorrow, what you can do today, because tomorrow is not promised." Mom has been asked to become a spokesperson for the cancer survivors network. She proudly accepted the invitation. She is preparing to travel next month to a cancer survivors convention in California. She will be their featured guest speaker.

Chapter Fourteen
Terry, Sr., Has A
Family Crisis

FOURTEEN

We received a call from Terry, Sr., he is the brother to my grandmother's deceased husband. His family was in crisis. Terry, Sr., and his family live in Atlanta, Georgia. Terry, Sr., had been married to his wife Mary for thirty years. Terry, Sr., was so proud of his children and his wife. They have two teenage children. His son Terry, Jr., seventeen and his daughter Marion, sixteen. Both are in high school dealing with typical teenage problems. Terry, Jr., is an honor roll student and he plays sports. He is looking forward to attending college on an athletic scholarship. He is level-headed and intelligent. Any father would be proud to call him, son. He has such a promising future. Terry, Jr., stands 6'4 with big brown eyes and a smile that could melt your heart if he gazed at you long enough. He is an immaculate dresser. He takes that after his father. He takes pride in the way he looks. He isn't like his peers who think it's cool to talk trash and have your pants sagging around your butt. He understands his appearance speaks volumes when job hunting or trying to impress a certain young lady and her family. He believes image is an important asset. He is being pursued by several young ladies, however, he doesn't accept their advances. He feels that it's a man's duty to pursue his soulmate, and not the other way around. Some duties and roles cannot be exchanged.

Terry, Jr., loves his baby sister, Marion. There is no sibling rivalry between them. He idolizes his sister. When she was sick, he got sick. When Marion got the measles, he took a red marker and put red spots on his face so she wouldn't feel alone.

Marion isn't your typical teenage girl. She loves to do boy things. She is a tomboy to her heart. She loves climbing trees, and jumping off any elevated surface. The dirtier she gets, the happier she is. Her mother has tried putting ribbons in her hair and dressing her in pink, but she hates it. She goes to great lengths to pull the ribbons out of her hair and to get her dresses filthy. Marion is short she is only 5'2' in stature. She has dark brown auburn hair. She has freckles on her face. Her hair is cut into a crew cut. If you saw her for the first time you would swear she was a boy. When Terry, Jr., and Marion are together you can't tell that they are of the opposite sex. She loves jeans and a big sweat shirt. No matter how hard her mother tried she couldn't make her act like a young lady. Her mother asked her what was wrong with being a young lady? Marion replied, its boring and she wants to have fun. Her mother threw up both hands as to surrender. Mary was exasperated with the situation.

Mary's world is built around her family. She is small in stature and a little on the heavy side, since she loves to cook and eat unhealthy foods. She has a very outgoing personality. She's very pretty and very feminine. Mary has a college degree, however she chose not to work outside her home. Her job is taking care of her family, which she takes great pride in doing.

Mary has a passion for interior decorating and will begin taking classes in the fall. Interior decorating is her God-given talent. She hopes one day to be able to open her own shop. She can't decide what to call her business for now it's just a dream that she hopes to make a reality in the near future. Her husband is encouraging her because he too believes she has the talent to become a great interior decorator. But he also wants to remove all her decorating things out of the basement and his garage. She has been storing things all over the house to be used in the future. She can't pass a garage sale without purchasing something. She's in heaven at a red tag sale. She is always willing to lend a helping hand to family and friend's. She feels it is a blessing to be able to lend a helping hand at something she enjoys doing.

Marion is taking driver's education which is required to get a license at sixteen. She is so excited about receiving her driving permit and license. Her mom is not happy about it. However, her father is encouraging her to do so. Her parents had no idea that receiving her license would change her life so drastically. She had her license for only two weeks when the car she was driving was forced off the road. The car landed in a ditch. She wasn't wearing her seat belt. She hit her head upon impact against the steering wheel. Her legs were pinned under the steering wheel. She had to be cut out of the car by the jaws of life. She was then rushed to Brady Memorial hospital in critical condition.

Mary was in the kitchen cooking dinner and there was a knock at the front door. When she looked out she saw two uniformed police officers. She immediately knew something was wrong. Mary felt faint and wasn't sure if she could make it to the front door. She called for her husband and her son. They both answered and came running to see what was wrong. Her husband got to the front door first and answered it. He too was shocked to see two police officers standing at their front door. Officer, "How may I help you?" The officer cleared his throat, "We are looking for the family of Marion Contour. She has been in a car accident. We are here to escort you to Brady Memorial Hospital." How is she? "We can't say, we just need to get you to the hospital as quickly as possible." He didn't say another word he just started getting his hat and coat and exited, with the whole family close on his heels. The family arrived at the hospital within minutes with a police escort. Upon arrival the family was asked to wait in the emergency waiting room. Mary was an emotional wreck. Terry, Jr., was silent and he seemed to be praying. Terry, Sr., was calm and focused. He too seemed to be in prayer and deep thought. The emergency room doctor came to the waiting room to speak with the family. "He informed them that Marion was in a deep coma and that he had done all that he could do. She's in God's hands now. She needs a lot of rest, and she will be feed through a tube until she regains consciousness. Once she regains consciousness we can evaluate how bad her head injury is. She could remain in a coma for days, weeks or even months. The brain is a very fragile and complex organ. We just have no way or determining what is happening in her brain. For now, we will just keep her comfortable and watch her vitals." Mary started to sob uncontrollably. Their son couldn't control himself any longer, he started shouting, "Oh' my God, can't you try something? There must be a test or something you can do besides watch her sleep. Where are the specialists? Where are the brain surgeons? You can't just leave her like that. Do something, please! We need her to get well." Before the doctor could reply, he broke down and cried in his father's arms. The doctor feeling helpless just shook his head. "Son, I'm sorry there's nothing more we can do." He then told the family that they could visit with Marion for a few brief moments." Marion's father thanked the doctor for all he had done. He then gathered the family into a circle. We held hands and he asked his wife to pray for Marion's healing and for strength for his family to grow closer in their hour of crisis. After things had settled down, friends and family began to leave the hospital. Terry, Sr., called our family in Ohio to share the heartbreaking news. Upon hearing the tragic news we all packed a bag and suitcase and headed to the airport.

Chapter Fifteen
Flight To Atlanta

FIFTEEN

Terry, Sr., greeted us at the airport and took us directly to the Brady Memorial Hospital. Although we had heard a lot about Terry's family and we had communicated over the phone, this was the first time the Washington's and Contour family had a face to face meeting. I felt sad that we were meeting under such sad circumstances.

When our family entered the hospital waiting room, we spotted Terry, Jr., immediately. He looked like a carbon copy of his father. Of course Marion's mother was sitting close by. Mary was struggling to hold herself together. But, she greeted us with a warm smile and a hug. This ordeal was taking a toil on Mary's health. Mary was a beautiful and happy woman usually. But this day, her eyes were blood shot from crying. She looked tired and in need of rest. She looked as if she could pass out any moment. I felt so sorry for her and the entire family. We all gathered in a circle and began to pray for the family and Marion. Once we finished praying in the waiting room, we went to Marion's hospital room. We gathered around her hospital bed and prayed again. This time it was my grandmother, who sent up a powerful prayer to God on Marion's behalf. My grandmother was a powerful woman of God who believed the prayers of the righteous availeth much. After we finished praying the doctor entered the room. Terry, Sr., began to question him about his daughter's condition. The doctor informed us that Marion was resting comfortably and he didn't believe she was in any pain. However, there had been no change in her condition.

It had been a stressful forty-eight hours since the accident, and the family hadn't left the hospital. We had eaten very little and sleep was all but non-existent. The entire family needed a hot bath and a meal. We decided to leave the hospital to get a bite to eat and freshen up. Terry, Sr., took us to his house. It was beautiful, something you would see in a magazine. Terry, Sr., worked as an engineer, and he helped to build his house, it was obvious money wasn't a problem.

Mary refused to join us for fear that something might happen while she was away. Terry, Sr., respected her wishes and left her in Marion's room. We felt guilty leaving her alone, however, it was a necessity. We returned a few hours later with food and a change of clothes for Mary. However, she was upset that we had left her alone and she refused to eat or drink anything. Terry, Sr., tried to reason with her, but with no avail. We went to the waiting room to give Terry, Sr., and his wife some privacy. This tugged at my heart, I felt so helpless, I wondered if their marriage was strong enough to survive this crisis. I could only pray that their marriage would survive. Before Marion's accident they seemed to be such a loving and happy couple. However, many marriage's have fallen apart because they could not handle the stress of the ilness. I pray with time they would find, that special love they once shared.

It had been four days. We had been vigilant and steadfast with our prayers, but Marion was still in a coma. The time had come for our departure. We had booked the flight for a five day return. Tomorrow our fifth day was upon us. We didn't want to leave while Marion was still in critical condition, but mom and my stepfather needed to get back to work and my brother needed to get back to school. My grandmother and I pondered whether we should stay, because we had nothing pressing to return home to. But, it was later decided we had done all we could do and that it would be costly to make changes to our flight itinerary. Early Saturday, morning we said our good-byes, hugged and kissed everyone and departed. But, not before my grandmother prayed a prayer that brought us all to tears. She called upon all prayer warriors who knew the power of prayer to pray daily for blessings and healing for Marion and her family.

Terry, Jr., took us to the airport and he thanked us for coming. It was a pleasant flight home, not much conversation. We were all in deep thought about the tragic turn of events, that we had just witnessed. It wasn't until I arrived home that I realized how much I had missed our little city. Atlanta, Georgia, was a nice place to visit, but I wouldn't want to live there. Once we were settled in my stepfather called Terry, Sr., to see if there had been any change in Marion's condition. Much to our disappointment there had not been. Terry, Sr., said, the doctor was concerned about Marion's lack of mobility causing bed sores. He ordered Marion to be placed on a special air mattress and he also ordered that she be turned to prevent bed sores from developing. This would also prevent muscle spasms. Terry, Sr., was satisfied that the doctor was doing everything in his power to make Marion comfortable. It had been a month since the accident and there had been little or no change. Terry, Sr., returned to work and Terry, Jr., returned to school. Mary sat faithfully by her daughter's bedside, refusing to leave. She is angry with her husband and son for going on with their lives. Mary has made visiting Marion uncomfortable for her husband and son. Often, she would say hateful things to them. The longer Marion lays lifeless and in the coma, the more Mary becomes despondent and hateful. Terry, Sr., doesn't know what to do. If he's there she's angry, and if he's not there she's angry. Marion's brother, is so distraught over his sister's declining health that he wants to drop out of school, of course his father won't hear of it.

My stepfather calls once a week to check on Marion's condition. With each call he sounded more and more desperate. His life had become a living nightmare, with no end insight. He is beginning to question God, He thinks God is punishing him for some sin he had committed in his past life. My stepfather tried to encourage him and to lift his spirits, but nothing seemed to be helping. Terry, Sr., was feeling stressed out and desperate. Not knowing what to do or which direction to turn, Terry, Sr., called his dear friend, my grandmother. My grandmother was pleasantly surprised to hear from him. She was worried about him and his family. She prayed for them daily asking God to heal them. He felt guilty for taking up so much of her time. He knew she led a busy lifestyle, and he wondered if he was keeping her from something important. After realizing they had been on the phone for hours. He apologized for taking up so much of her time. My grandmother laughed, at him she had enjoyed talking with him. She was never too busy to talk with her family or friends. Before she ended the phone call my grandmother prayed again for him and his family. She bowed her head and began to pray such a sweet and melodious prayer that it brought tears to his eyes. He was glad that she couldn't see his face as he wiped tears that were rolling down his cheeks. After talking with her he felt as if weights had been lifted off his shoulders. He said, "Good night, he ended the call feeling at peace."

Chapter Sixteen
Marion's Health Declines

SIXTEEN

Everyone's life was happy and progressing as planned except for Terry, Sr., and his family. Terry, Sr., and Mary were having serious martial problems because of their daughter's health problems. Marion had been in a coma for the past year. Mary stopped living the day their daughter was admitted into the hospital. Nothing her husband had said, or tried had put their marriage back on track. Mary had taken up residence at the hospital. It's as if she had forgotten she had a husband and a son who needed her desperately. Nothing and no one seems to be able to get through to her. She's mad at the world. When her husband goes to the hospital, they do nothing, but fight and argue. It got so bad one night that the hospital security was contacted to intervene for fear of someone getting hurt. Her son had tried to reason with his mother, but with no success. He poured out his heart to his mother telling her how much he missed having her in his life. He still loved and needed her to be a mother to him. His pleading fell on deaf ears. He left the hospital vowing never to return because it was just too painful for him to watch the two women he loved so deeply just waste away. He was so depressed about his mother and sister's condition that he sought relief in a bottle of whiskey. He started staying out nights drinking with his buddies, coming in at all hours of the night. One night he was in the wrong place at the wrong time, and he was mugged and beaten. He had to be hospitalized because the mugger broke his arm. He only had one-hundred dollars in his wallet, and this made the mugger mad. The police officer who took the report stated that he was lucky to be alive. The last individual, who got mugged in the same location wasn't so lucky. His funeral was being held that day. All he had on him was fifty dollars. He left behind two children and a wife. The officer also suggested that if he felt the need to drink he should do it at home because it was much safer. Terry Jr., assured the officer his drinking days were over. He had learned a valuable lesson. He never touched alcohol again not even for special ocassions.

Marion was released from the hospital only to be admitted to a nursing home where she would spend the remainder of her days. Placing Marion in a nursing home sent Mary off the deep end. Mary had to be placed in a psychiatric facility. It broke her husband's heart to see her in such a neurotic state. He felt guilty about placing her there but, he had no choice. Mary had made a conscience choice to slip away into the darkness. Nothing and no one mattered to her now. It was just heartbreaking to see their family being torn apart. Terry, Sr., turned to his sister-law for guidance and comfort. Since David's death the friendship with his brother had grown stronger. Her strength had helped him to survive his family crisis.

The nursing home that Marion was to be placed in was Briarcliff Haven Healthcare and Rehabilitation Center. The nursing home came highly recommended by the social worker and a few close friends. Briarcliff Haven Healthcare and Rehabilitation Center had been the leader in providing care for seniors in the Atlanta area. Briarcliff Haven is located on twenty-five acres of beautifully landscaped grounds with walkways, covered shelters and easily accessible decks and courtyard areas for family, and friends to enjoy. Terry, Sr., went to visit several nursing homes before deciding to place Marion there. Once he made the decision and filled out the necessary paperwork, he went to talk with his son. He expected his son to be in full agreement with placing his sister in this facility, however; he was gravely mistaken. His son didn't like the nursing home or its location. In fact, he didn't want his sister placed in a nursing home. He wanted his sister brought home. He felt she deserved to be taken care of by family and not some stranger. Terry, Sr., was surprised to hear these words coming out of his son's mouth. He tried to explain to his son that he too wanted Marion to have the best of care. But, he didn't feel they had the necessary medical knowledge to care for her. His father suggested they visit other nursing facilities if he didn't like the location that had been chosen. Terry, Jr., paced the floor, "Yelling, this just wasn't fair. His sister should not be laying in a hospital or nursing home, its just not fair! Why, why did God allow this to happen to her?" Marion should be in college having the time of her life. Terry, Jr., looked his dad, in the face and again, yelled, "Why? Why do bad things happen to good people?" The person who ran her off the road is able to go on with their life without being punished for their wrong doing. His father sat in silence, while his son cried and paced the floor. He understood his son frustrations. Unfortunately he didn't have an answers for his son. He was at a loss for words, so he continued to sit quietly. He knew his son was hurting and he wanted to comfort him. He stood to his feet and moved toward his son. He wanted to hug him and to tell him everything was going to be alright. However, that couldn't be farther from the truth. He knew that things would get worse as time passed. Once they placed Marion in a nursing home, the next big dilemma was what to do with his wife. Terry, Sr., decided to face one dilemma at a time. The first decision was where to place Marion. He needed his son to be in agreement with him. To place Marion in the Briarcliff Haven Healthcare and Rehabilitation Center. This was not a easy decison for either of them to make. They both wanted what was best for her. It would take time to adjust to this new arrangement.

Once his son settled down his father questioned him again about the nursing home. Terry, Jr., agreed that her heath issues would be to much for them to handle. He gave his consent to place Marion in the nursing home and his mother in the state facility. He didn't like the idea of placing them there but he knew this was the best places for them both.

Chapter Seventeen
Terry, Sr., Faces A Dilemma

SEVENTEEN

Terry's heart was heavy over his wife and daughter's condition. He wanted so much to change what had occurred. However, that would take a miracle. A miracle that only God could deliver. For now, that miracle just wasn't happening. If prayers and tears could change the circumstances he would have gladly exchanged places with them. He believed in the power of prayer, and he was a praying man. However, he had to question God as to why this was happening to him and to his family. He also wondered what was he to do with his life since two of the most important people in his life were now confined to hospital beds.

He was a deeply distraught man. A part of him felt guilty about moving on with his life without them. However, a little voice in his head told him it was okay to live his life and to be happy. He didn't know if he should listen to that little voice whispering in his ear. No matter what he did he felt guilty. He spent his days working and his nights between the nursing home and the hospital. He wasn't sleeping at night so when daylight hit he felt tired and sleepy. He spent many agonizing nights on his knees praying and asking God to show him what he should do. The answer he prayed for was not revealed unto him. He felt so helpless. He was an emotional wreck and he needed help. He contacted his pastor. His pastor offered him words of comfort that left him even more confused. He told him to continue to pray and that God would give him an answer. He left the counseling session feeling even more helpless. He shared his feeling with sister-in-law. She also told him to continue praying and God would send him an answer. He was greatful for their prayers and words of comfort. However, he needed something a little more precise in order to relieve his despression and guilt.

Not getting any rest or sleep started to affect his work. His partner asked to speak to him in private. He knew this was not going to be a friendly meeting. Terry, Sr., was an engineer and held 80% of the stock in the company. However, he still had a partner and stock holders to answer to if the company's rating or stocks took a fall. He walked into his partners office and took a seat. Just as he thought his partner wasn't smiling. His partner had this very serious and troubling look on his face. He cleared his throat, "Terry, I'm worried about you. You're not focused and it's showing in your work.

The firm thinks you need to take a leave of absence, just until you get some rest and make a few decisions about your family problems." Terry, Sr., just listened with his head down. He wasn't angry or upset, he knew his partner had his best interest at heart. Terry, Sr., stood to his feet and looked his partner in the face. "I'll think about your suggestions. I don't know if time off from work will help or hurt my situation." He thanked his partner for his concern and slowly left his office. His partner's suggestions only added to his worries. He gathered his personal belongings and left his office with a heavy heart. He was hurt and even more confused. He felt all alone with no one to turn to for help. Not knowing what to do or whom to turn to Terry, Sr., pulled out his cell phone and called his son. Just maybe his son could help him make a life changing decision. The phone rang for several seconds and then went into his voice mail. He just stared at the phone, disappointed that his son hadn't answered. He decided to end the call without leaving a message. He wasn't sure what he would have said if his son had answered. He looked to the heavens and cried out loud, "Lord, I need You to help me, I can't do this without You". He wanted to do what was best for his wife and daughter. However, what ever decisions he made someone would be unhappy, someone would be hurt. He didn't want to be selfish, or to hurt the two people he loved the most. However he couldn't keep going on this way with no sleep and no peace. He picked up his cell phone again, this time to call his sister-in-law. She had been his lifeline since his life started falling apart. His sister-in-law always knew the right words to encourage him, when he was troubled or low in spirit. Once again, the phone rang and rang for what seemed like hours, and then it went into voice mail. He desperately needed to hear her voice, to hear her say everything was going to be alright. But, no such luck. He would have to wait for another time. He was now sitting in his car just starring out the window. Wondering why and how his life had taken such a tragic turn. His mind began to reflect back to the good old days when the kids were in school, and he and Mary were so happy. Tears began to roll down his checks. He didn't wipe them. He just let them fall into his lap. He knew tears wouldn't solve his problems however, releasing the tears seemed to release some of his pent up frustrations. The sun was beginning to set in the west. He had lost track of time. he didn't know how long he had been sitting in his car. As the sun began to set he began to pray again. "Oh' God it's me again, "I come asking you to restore my joy and restore my peace in the name of Jesus. I know You said in your word that you wouldn't put more on me than I could bear, but God I can't stand this burden any longer. God I need you to step in and take control. Mend and heal their broken bodies. Give me the strength to carry on, to do Your will God. I can't do this without You." As he was praying, he was interrupted by the ringing of his phone. He jumped startled by the noise. He laughed at himself for allowing the phone to make him jump. He answered his phone and was happy to hear his son's voice on the other line. "I'm sorry I missed your call dad.. How are you? What's going on?"

He took a deep breath, "I just need someone to talk to. I am feeling a little down and out about a few things that have happened at work today.However, I'm feeling a little better now that I've talked to God. I still don't have all the answers, but I do feel better." There was silence on the phone, then, "Is there anything that I can do to help you dad?" There was another moment of silence on the phone while he collected his thoughts. Before he could respond, Terry, Jr., interrupted his father's thoughts and invited him over to his house so they could discuss the problems in person. "How long will it take you to get here? Only twenty minutes, then it's settled I'll see you in twenty minutes or less." He put the car in drive and headed for his son's home. He was feeling relieved that he had someone to talk to. He was happy he was going to spend some quality time with his son. As he drove he reflected back on his son's success. Time was moving swiftly, his son was a grown man with a family of his own. He had graduated from Spelman College with a degree in graphic designs. He married his college sweetheart. They were expecting their first child in a few months. His son was a successful businessman and they lived in the suburbs of Atlanta, Georgia. His home also looked like a mansion you would find in a magazine "Homes of the Rich and Famous". The house had eight bedrooms and four baths and the backyard sat on a 15-acre estate. He was a proud of his son and all he had.accomplished. He pulled into his son's driveway, his son stood in the doorway with a worried look on his face. He greeted his father with a smile and a big hug. The first words out of his mouth were, "Dad what's wrong? His father cleared his throat and attempted to answer him. "I don't know where to start, "Take your time dad and start at the beginning." He slowly began to share what was troubling him. His son listened, and was amazed at what he was hearing. Once his father finished, Terry, Jr., hugged his father again. "Dad you do need to take a leave of absence to handle your affairs." He understood his desire to care of his mother and sister. However, he had done all that he could do to help them. Now it's time for him to move on with his life. He could no longer afford to spend every waking moment at the nursing home or the hospital. He had been a good husband and father. Divorcing his mom wouldn't be easy. However, it was necessary. He gave his father the name of a good divorce attorney. He even offered to call and make an appointment for him. However, his father declined the offer. He didn't feel comfortable allowing his son to handle this matter. This was something he needed to handle, after all he was the adult and the father. He thanked his son and assured him he could take care of this matter himself.

Chapter Eighteen
A New Birth

EIGHTEEN

The divorce attorney that his son had recommended was one of the best attorney's in the state. Within months, he was holding his divorce decree in his hand. However, he was still having problems accepting the fact that he was a divorced man. He thought having his divorce decree would make him feel better. However, even with his divorce decree in his hand he was still wondering if he had done the right thing. He just kept staring at the divorce decree. Reading it over and over again. He felt as if he had abandoned his family. He felt that somehow this was all his fault. Maybe if he had stood firm on not allowing Marion to drive at sixteen, things would have turned out differently. But how could he have known that his decision would change their lives forever? That's just it, he couldn't have foreseen the future. So even though he felt guilty, it wasn't his fault. He had been married to Mary for almost thirty years. They grew up in the same neighborhood and attended the same elementary and high school. They even attended the same college so they could continue their romance. Once they graduated from college they got married the very next day. Every good or bad memory included Mary. Now, how was he suppose to start a new life without her? His son felt he should. "Get a divorce and move on with his life. But, how was he suppose to do that? The divorce decree released him from his legal obligation. However, he still felt strongly connected to his now ex-wife. He still thought about her day and night. He still loved her and worried about her health. He still felt compelled to visit her everyday, and he did just that. So really had anything changed? He wondered why Mary couldn't just make a conscience choice to be well, therefore, healing herself? But, the doctors had told him that Mary's illness was not just emotional. The doctor felt "At some point and time, Mary had suffered an aneurysm which damaged her brain beyond repair. With the stress of her daughter's injury and the affect of the aneurysm, it was more then her body could handle. He knew the doctors diagnosis. However, that didn't stop him from wishing his wife and daughter to be whole again. He wanted to turn back the hands of time. It had been over a year since his daughter's accident. Shortly afterwards his wife had been committed to a mental institute. Marion's condition had not changed either due to her brain injury. All he could think about was how unfair this was that both the women in his life had been taken away from him. He knew he shouldn't question God's will for his life. However, this day he couldn't help but asked God, "Why? Why my family?" He again started to pray. He asked God to help him accept His will and to give him understanding. He felt exhausted and weary. He closed his eyes hoping sleep would come. Just as he drifted off to sleep his phone rang. He looked at the caller ID and decided not to answer the call and to let it go into his voice mail. He was sure his son was calling to check up on him and invite him to dinner. He just didn't feel up to talking. He just wanted to get some much needed rest. He would return his phone call after his nap. He closed his eyes again and drifted off to sleep. When he awoke much to his surprise, he had slept for over two hours. While he slept he dreamed of Mary and the kids in their younger years. They were happy and having such a good time at the state fair. His dream seemed so real that he didn't want to wake up. He sat on the edge of the bed smiling and reminiscing over the good old days. The memories faded quickly and reality hit him in his face when he looked at the divorce decree on the top of his nightstand. Back to the reality, that his life would never be that way again. He felt sad over the loss of his ideal marriage and perfect family. He hated having idle time on his hands to reflect on what was, and what he would never have again. Night time was the worse, either he couldn't sleep or if he did he had the same recurring dream of the happy family he once had. The dream was a painful reminder of his loss. He shook his head and wondered if things would ever get better.

He stood to his feet to leave his bedroom. He needed a change of scenery. His cell phone had a blinking light which reminded him that hiis son had tried to call him. He picked up the phone to return his call. Then he ended the call abruptly, and decided to pay his son a visit. He really needed to get out of his apartment. He needed to smell the fresh air and to be with family. He jumped into his car and headed to his son's home. Upon arrival, he noticed a note pinned to the door. He jumped out of his car and ran to read the note. The note read "If you're looking for Terry, Jr., and family we are on our way to the hospital to deliver our first born child. You are welcome to join us at Brady Memorial Hospital. If you can't join us, please pray for a healthy baby. Proud Parents"! Mr. & Mrs. Contour

With a smile on his face, Terry's heart started racing and he started jumping up and down. This was the best news he had heard in years. A new addition to the family. He was going to be a grandfather. The reality had not set in the past nine months. Now it was real to him. Terry, Sr., couldn't get to the hospital fast enough. He thought for sure he was going to be stopped by the police and given a ticket. He was speeding and driving recklessly. But he couldn't wait to get to the hospital. He didn't want to miss the birth of his first grandchild. He smiled and thought, if I get a ticket it will be worth it. He would gladly take the ticket and continue speeding to the hospital. He had to laugh at the thought. Much to his surprise, he made it to the hospital without getting a ticket. He parked the car and started running toward the maternity ward. A guard at the desk stopped him. "Sir, can I help you?" "Yes, my son is having a baby. The guard laughed, sir, your son is having a baby? You mean your son's wife is having a baby?" "Yes, yes, can you tell me where to find my son and his wife." Terry Contour Jr., wait just one moment, sir. They are in room 3220 on the third floor." He arrived just in time to see his daughter-in-law deliver a healthy 7lb.' 8oz baby girl. This was indeed one of the happiest moments of his life. His son named their first born after his sister Marion. Terry, Sr., felt as though this new birth was a sign that it was okay to move on with no regrets. He felt emotions he hadn't felt since the birth of his own children. His son placed his newborn daughter in his father's arms. Everyone gathered around as he began to pray over the new addition to his family. "He thanked God for blessing them with this bundle of joy, and he asked God to always keep her safe and to show her favor. He thanked God for all the many blessings He had given to his family. Then he paused for a minute, Father, if it be Your will restore Mary and Marion to good health. In the name of Your son Jesus. Amen. Everyone repeated in unison, amen! The nurse entered the room to inform everyone that visiting hours were over and that the new mother needed to get some rest. Everyone understood and they gathered their belongings. to leave. Terry, Sr., couldn't wait to share the good news with family and friends. Once outside, he dialed his sister-in-laws cell phone. Again she didn't answer. It went into her voice mail. He wondered where could she be. Thinking of her brought a smile to his face. He got into his car to return to his apartment. Hoping she would return his call soon, so he could share his good news..

Chapter Nineteen
Terry, Sr., Finds Peace

NINETEEN

Terry, Sr., entered his apartment with a sense of contentment he hadn't felt in years. He couldn't believe how the birth of this new child had changed his life. He looked forward to returning to work. He couldn't wait for the new baby and mother to be discharged from the hospital so he could visit them. He looked forward to babysitting and to shopping for toys for his little angel. As he sat day dreaming about the new addition to his family, his cell phone rang. He checked his caller ID. It was his sister-in-law returning his phone call. He was so excited to hear from her he couldn't sit still. He started pacing the floor when he heard her voice. She could tell from the excitement in his voice that he had good news to share. She waited patiently for him to share his good news Finally, after questioning her about her day and listening patiently. He interrupted her,"God is so good, he has blessed my family with a new baby." My son and his wife just gave birth to a little girl.. Mother and child are resting comfortably and will be discharged tomorrow. She weighed 7lb.' 8oz, and she's so beautiful. She looks just like my daughter Marion. He felt proud that they had named the baby Marion. He couldn't wait for his sister-in-law to see this bundle of joy who had changed his life. He didn't have all the details for the baptism yet. However, he believed she would be baptized next month. He hoped the family would come to share in this special occasion. He hadn't call my stepfather or my mother yet. However, he was going to share the good news and invite us to come once he hung up the phone. Before he hung up the phone he questioned his sister-in-law as to whether she would be able to attend? She replied that wild horses couldn't keep her away. Once the details were finalized she asked him to call her. When she received the final details she would make sure her calendar was clear so that she and the family could attend. She was happy to hear the good news, However, she was even happier to hear him so excited. She hoped this would be a life changing event for him and it was. Terry, Sr., and my grandmother were communicating by phone daily. She looked forward to his calls. Each day he had exciting news about his granddaughter. He talked about the first time he fed her and sang her to sleep. He shared the first time he gave her a bath and tucked her into bed, and the list just kept growing. It was as if he had never done these things before. It has been said, being a grandparent is God's gift. Because what ever you didn't get a chance to do right as a parent, as a grandparent you have a chance to correct it.

Terry, Sr., certainly was taking advantage of the opportunity. He was enjoying every moment of being a grandparent. This child would not want for anything her grandpa, would see to it that she had everything her heart wanted or desired. Nothing was to expensive or off limits for his new grandbaby.

My grandmother searched daily for more information regarding the baptism. She went to her mail box and finally she found an envelop with an return address of Atlanta, Georgia. She quickly opened it. It was an invitation to the baptism and to a dinner for baby Marion. My grandmother quickly picked up the phone to call my mother to see if they had received their invitation. Yes, mom had received their invitation. Mom and my grandmother chatted for a while then, said their goodbyes. My grandmother contacted her brother-in-law to let him know when we would be arriving. We were all excited about going to Atlanta and seeing the new baby.

As the baptismal grew closer, the new grandfather became even more excited. He couldn't stop talking about the baptism and his family coming from Ohio. He made reservations at the Westin Hotel for the entire family. He picked us up from the airport. Upon arrival, he took us to our hotel and then he drove us to the church where the baptism was to be held. Everyone look so beautiful dressed in their Sunday best. Little Marion and her parent's were all dressed in white attire. Little Marion was now one month old. She looked so cute in her white gown and cap. She didn't like wearing the cap and she kept trying to pull it off. But, it was snapped under her chin. Her shoes were white with matching tights. Little Marion was in her grandfather's arms and wouldn't let anyone else touch her. The baptism was held at Ebenezer Baptist Church in Atlanta, Georgia. A beautiful church with some powerful history behind it. Upon entering we heard the powerful, peaceful, and biblical words of a great man named Martin Luther King Jr. co-pastor, from 1960-1968. His message played continuously and it resonated off the beautiful original stained glass windows of our nation's greatest church, community and the state. The proud grandfather was so excited about the baptism and the new baby, that he sent out invitations to everyone he knew and some he didn't know, just a friend of a friend. He wanted to share his good news and joy with everyone.

The pastor of the church, Rev. Dr. Raphael Gamaliel Warnock, started the ceremony by asking all the family members to come and stand beside the father and mother of little Marion. My stepfather and mom were appointed as the godparents by the proud parents. Then he began to explain the purpose for today's baptism: "Baptism can be defined as the sacrament of supernatural rebirth or regeneration. We should stress the prefix "re" when we speak of baptism as a rebirth or regeneration. This brings out the astounding fact that although we are indeed generated or born naturally of our human parents baptism gives us a new life. This is a higher life the supernatural life that we need above our natural existence. Why do we need this life? Because we hope to reach heaven after our natural life expires when we die. Absolutely speaking, none of us will ever die. What we commonly call death is merely the separation of our immortal soul from our earthly bodies. But the soul is meant to be alive twice over. As a spiritual reality, our soul will never cease to exist. But if our soul is not animated by the grace we received at baptism, we shall die the double death of both body and soul. He then took baby Marion in his arm,"We baptize you in the name of the Father, the Son and the Holy Ghost. Then he began to pray. He charged everyone within the sound of his voice to help rear this child in his arms. Because an old AFRICAN PROVERBS, says, "It takes a whole village to raise a child"! So if you agree to help these parents, please raise your hands and say I do! You must know these are difficult times to be rearing a child, and they will indeed need your assistance Rev. Dr. Raphael Gamaliel Warnock thanked everyone for coming and ended the service. As I looked around the church some people were crying.. It was such a touching service that it brought tears to my eyes. Once the service was over our family and friends gathered in the fellowship hall to eat and to take pictures. As I watched the family, I thanked God for this peace and happiness. I also prayed that we would be repeating this event one day soon. With my brother and his wife or with me and Greg.

Once the festivities were over Terry, Sr., and and son

offered to take us back to the hotel. My grandmother, mom and my stepfather rode with Terry, Sr., Everyone else got into Terry, Jr's truck. We continued to laugh and make fun of little moments that seemed funny to us all. The adults had a different conversation going on in their vehicle. My stepfather asked Terry, Sr., about his wife and daughter. "Things hadn't changed much in the last couple of years. He offered to take them to the nursing home and to the hospital. At first everyone seemed to agree that it wasn't a good idea. However, mom didn't feel comfortable coming this far and not visiting for a short while. Terry, Sr., called to instruct us that they were making a quick stop and that we should continue on to the hotel. We didn't asked any questions. We just continued to the hotel.

Terry, Sr., stopped his car in front of this tall white building. The adults went to visit with Mary first. Then they continued the journey to visit with Marion Each visit was short because neither were responsive, they were both in a vegetative state. They left feeling helpless and sad. However, they knew God was in control and there was nothing else any of them could do, but pray. Before they left they said a prayer asking that God's will be done. They returned to the car in silence each person deep in thought about what they had just seen.

Chapter Twenty
Terry, Sr., and Gwen Find Love

TWENTY

The ride back to the hotel was silent with only music playing from the radio to comfort them. Once they arrived at the hotel my stepfather and mom got out of the car and went directly to their hotel. They exchanged a few brief words only to say good night. I believe mom regretted suggesting that they go to visit Mary and Marion. Although it did set her mind at rest as to how they were doing. My grandmother watched as mom and my stepfather exited the car. However, my grandmother didn't move. She was searching for words to comfort her friend. At that very moment, she realized how much she cared about him. Over the years she denied having feeling for him. But today she could no longer deny her feelings, because she was feeling his pain deeply.

She said a silent prayer asking God to give her the words to comfort her friend. He had found God which brought peace and happiness into his life. It wasn't fair that after struggling so hard to find peace and happiness that it should be taken away. After all, the events that had happened were not his fault. My grandmother wanted so much to comfort her friend. However, she couldn't seem to find the right words. After searching for what seemed like hours, she did the only thing she knew to do. She took his hand and started to pray, speaking to God on his behalf. She prayed, "Father in heaven we thank You for this day, and the many blessings You have given us. Now, we asked that You restore the joy and peace to my brother, my friend. Let him know that You love him and understand his pain. You want him to have perfect peace. Remind him that You are in control and this was Your will. Give him understanding and peace be returned unto him. Give him strength to accept Your will and to move on with his life."After my grandmother finished praying she reached over to hug him. He embraced her also. They just hugged each other forgetting about who could be watching them and their location. For one moment, the world seemed to stand still. The next thing that happened truly caught my grandmother off guard, but she didn't resist. He went from hugging her to kissing her lips. It was a surprise, but it felt natural. It felt good. It felt like she had done this before maybe in her dreams.They kissed for five minutes or more.Then my grandmother pulled away. She pulled away even though she liked the kiss. She began to wonder if what they were doing was right. They both sat quietly for a few minutes. Then, he broke the silence. "Did my kissing you offend you?" My grandmother only smiled, "No, I'm not upset. However, I have to wonder if what we're doing is right. "He started to apologize, but my grandmother stopped him. "There's no need to apologize. We are both consenting adults. We have been friends and family it seems like forever. We have shared the best of times and the worst of times. However, she felt a need to slow things down a little. To think about the consequences of their actions. The next words out of his mouth left her speechless. He confessed that he always had feelings for her just not on this level. His feelings had grown over the years. But because of his commitment, he knew he shouldn't and couldn't act on his feelings. However, now that things had changed so drastically over the last year or so she was the only woman he thought or dreamed about. He wasn't going to act on his feeling. However, when she hugged him he couldn't help himself. He just loss control. He told her how lonely he had been and how just hearing her voice brought peace and happiness into his life. He shared just how much their late night conversations helped him make it through each day. My grandmother listened quietly not knowing what to say. He continued to share how the past year she had been his whole reason for living. Many nights he had thought about taking his own life and the phone would ring and it would be her. He believed that this was God intervening on his behalf because he was at the end of his rope. Now, he needed and wanted to share the rest of his ife with her. He told her she didn't have to answer him now. He just wanted her to think about it and to give him an answer before she left town. My grandmother and the family were scheduled to leave that next afternoon. He continued to say that he felt he had a lot of love to share, and secretly hoped one day that she would allow him to play an important role in her life. My grandmother just kept smiling and listening to every word that was coming out of his mouth. At one point she wondered if she was dreaming. But, that question was answered when again she felt his lips on hers.

This time she didn't stop him she just enjoyed the moment. When the kiss was over my grandmother took his hand and said that,"She didn't need anymore time to think about where this relationship was headed. Because she too had strong feelings for him and wanted to spend her twilight years with him. My grandmother kissed him and then said goodnight. She returned to her hotel room to pack for her flight home. My grandmother was feeling content that things would work out and that he would be a permanent fixture in her life.

Epilogue:

Terry, Sr., was true to his word. He asked my grandmother for her hand in marriage, my grandmother said, "Yes". The following year they eloped to Las Vegas, Nevada to be married. They spent one week on their honeymoon. They returned at the end of the week and had a large reception for family and friends who wanted to wish them well and share in their happiness. Once the festivities were over Gwen and her new husband packed her belongs and moved to Atlanta, Georgia to start their new life. She felt sad at leaving her family, but she had given them many years of her life. Now, it was time to take care of herself and her new husband.

Terry, Jr., and his wife are starting a new business. Assistant Living for senior citizens. They are still happily married and they now have two beautiful children.

Daniel, Sr., and Destiny have now retired and are volunteering in the community. Destiny is still active with her Cancer survivors group.

My brother and his wife are expecting their second child. Hope and her husband, Greg, are purchasing their first home and are working on having their first child.

Other books published by
Toles Publishing House:

Doug Toles "Original Gospel Songs"
"The Greatest Gift"
"Don't Wait Too Late"

Evangelist Audrey Green
"When Love Hurts, I'm A Survivor"
Marie Edley
"In God's Hands"
Delores Earley
"The Answer"
Anna Gee Blackwell
"He's All I Need, My Life Story!

www.dougtoles.com
www.daytonchristianwriters.com

Other books written by Author:

Perfect Peace

Life's Lessons

Finding Hope

Raising Hope

Whispers From Above

Anthology Of Ohio Poets

Perfect Peace Prayer Journal

Reflections Of The Heart And Soul

www.dougtoles.com

Daytonwriters@ureach.com

www.Daytonchristianwriters.com

**Books written by members of the
Dayton Christian Writers' Guild Inc.
Suggested Reading:**

Rev. David Elkins
"Fallen Stars"
Rev. Rita Bryant
"The Family"
Christina Tellis
"Built This Way"
Howard Ross
 "We Are Still Here"
Scott Fortune
"Fasley Accused"
 Catherine Myrick
"Vengeance of War"
Justine Nettleton
"Arise and Shine"
Dr. Eugenia Gumm
"Amazing Bible Treasure"
 Evangelist Audrey Green
"A Daddy's Love"
"So You Thought You Had Me"
 "When Love Hurts, I'm A Survivor"
Nikol Boddie-Treece
"Power Ushering Students Higher"
"Steps For Success"

Leslie Nwanoro
"Avoiding Pitfalls &
Fortifying The Walls Of Marriage"
Christine Devlin
"God Is A Horseman"
Judith Dammons
"So What Now God"

"Raising Hope"
Regaining Hope
Finding Hope

If you wish to purchase additional books
Please send a list of requested titles and a check to:
Mrs. Tina Toles
863 Sunset Drive
Englewood, Ohio 45322
937-836-6600
$15.00 per book plus $3.00 dollars shipping
& Handling fees:
Books may also be purchased online at:
www.amazon.com
or
www.daytonchristianwriters.com

About The Author

Mrs. Toles resides in Englewood, Ohio with her husband, Douglas. They have a blended family of six children, eight grandchildren, and ten great grandchildren whom they adore. Mrs. Toles is retired from the Northmont City Schools.

Mrs. Toles is the Founder/President of the Dayton Christian Writers' Guild Inc. and the co-owner of Toles Publishing House.

Mrs. Toles seeks to aid all writers who have a desire to "Write For God's Glory". She truly believes there's at least one book in all of us.

Mrs. Toles has written three books of poetry, "Reflections of The Heart and Soul", "Anthology Of Ohio Poets" and "Whispers From Above."

Mrs. Toles has also written, a self-help book for Christians, "Perfect Peace and A Prayer Journal" to support Christians on this journey.

"Finding Hope" "Raising Hope" and "Regaining Hope" is the final novel in this sequel.

Mrs. Toles next endeavor will be "Words of Wisdom" to be complete the summer of 2017.

www.ingramcontent.com/pod-product-compliance
Lightning Source LLC
Chambersburg PA
CBHW060119260626
47160CB00005B/1938